When Love Returns

The Star Lake Series: Book One

Lorana Hoopes

Acknowledgements

Special thanks to Kathy S. who reads and gives me feedback along the way. Also to my Street Team – Earthly Angels who I know will do a great job helping me promote this book. I'd also like to thank the students in my Stunning Stories class who continue to inspire me with their great imaginations and wonderful stories.

Dedication

This book is dedicated first and foremost to my husband who lets me write in the evenings and to my children – I'll never write something I'd be ashamed to show you. Also to Brandon M., thank you for being my muse.

Table of Contents

Chapter One - Brandon Returns

*T*here it is. The one stoplight I thought I'd never see again, still blinking its irregular red pattern that no one ever paid attention to. As most of the shops are centrally located, few people drive in town. Their cars are used for driving to neighboring cities when what they want isn't available here, so there is no real need for the stop light, but the people had decided the town needed at least one stoplight to be called a proper town, and so it had been erected.

There had been a huge ceremony the day it was christened; the whole town had shown up. The mayor had had to stand on a ladder to cut the red ribbon as someone had placed it too high. Once he was up the ladder, another member of the city board had handed him a giant pair of silver scissors. Then it had become a balancing act as the mayor tried to open the giant scissors without losing his balance – that had been comical – and we had watched in awe as it blinked, blinked, long pause, blinked, blinked. The awe had faded quickly, and a squabble had broken out among the adults about the broken light. The whole affair had been rather disappointing to a sixteen-year-old, who had been looking forward to getting his driver's license, and I remembered that day as the nail in the coffin solidifying my idea of leaving this tiny backwards town and returning to normalcy.

Then I met Presley, and my life changed.

"Are we there yet, Daddy?"

I glance in the rearview mirror at my daughter, Joy, strapped in her car seat. Her dark curls came from me, but her blue-grey eyes are her mother's. Joy is the one good thing that came out of this town.

"Almost, Pumpkin."

She resumes her stare out the window as we continue down Main Street. The Diner still sits on the corner, probably still run by Max, the same uninspired owner who wore a ball cap and plaid flannel shirt to work every day. His choice of attire left a lot to be desired, but he was a good cook. To this day, I'm not sure I've had a better burger.

Next to the diner is the small Post Office. I never spent much time in it growing up, but I knew the man who worked there, Bert. He was an odd man to say the least – always trying out new ideas that never seemed to work. One year, he had tried raising chickens to supply eggs for the general store, but he had become attached to one of the chickens, naming her Stella and carrying her from place to place in a little bag like wealthy old women do with tiny dogs. The chicken had escaped the bag one day in the middle of The Diner and wreaked havoc, incensing Max. Stella disappeared after that, and I was fairly certain she ended up on Max's menu, but I could never prove it.

The general store appears next. It carries groceries and a small selection of clothing and household goods. I had been shocked by the meager selection when I first arrived, but the town wears on you and has a way of making you forget the outside world moving on around it. By the time I graduated high school, I had been accustomed to the small offerings until I arrived in Dallas and felt like a total hick, at least three years behind the times.

"Daddy, look, cupcakes. Can we get one?"

Twisting in the black leather seat, I follow her finger pointing out the opposite window. There had been no cupcake shop six years ago, but there is indeed a shop there now, where the laundromat had been, sporting a colorful cupcake sign and logo on the window. Sweet Treats. It's not a highly original name, but neither are most of the stores in this town.

"We'll come back by later." I am curious about the owner. Who would choose to put up a new shop in this sleepy little town?

Her bottom lip turns out in an adorable pout, but she does not continue to fight me. For her, this trip is like a vacation to a new and unusual place. We rarely venture from Dallas, mainly because my work keeps me too busy for vacations. For me, it's a return to a past I want to forget. There's too much pain, too much sadness here in this little town.

I make a right down Cooper Street, the road that leads to my parent's house. Though it has been years since I have been back here, I could drive the route blindfolded, partly because it is a simple route, and partly because I walked it so many times as a teenager.

The two-story yellow house looks exactly as I remember it, though the paint is chipping in a few more places and faded in others. The gravel of the driveway crunches under the tires as I pull in. I park the car and take a deep breath.

"Let me out Daddy," Joy calls from the back seat.

Sighing, I open my door and then reach in to unbuckle her. Though five, she is still too small to qualify for a booster seat, and I feel safer having her in the bigger car seat anyway. No one ever told me that when I became a parent, I would have crazy nightmares about all the ways I could lose my daughter. The car accident is always the worst.

Joy scurries out of the car, her faded pink bunny clutched in one petite hand. On the day she was born, my mother had given her a soft pink cuddle bunny. Joy had latched onto it, sleeping with it every night. When she began crawling, she would often pick up the bunny in her mouth, dragging it across the floors. Even after she began walking, the bunny would go outside with her to play in the dirt or be flung around the room. The bunny has seen better days, but she refuses to part with it for any longer than an occasional trip in the washing machine, and of course, no one sells this bunny any longer. I dread the day when it falls apart and I can't replace it.

As she scrambles up the wooden porch, I pop the trunk and grab the two suitcases I packed the night before. My hope is that we'll only be here a week, but I have no guarantee and therefore packed for at least two.

Joy is banging on the door when I reach her side. She hasn't been around my parents much, as we left shortly after her first birthday, but they did visit a few times and Joy always clung to them when they did as if she knew the time wouldn't be for very long. Now, she has created this idea in her head of what they'll be like while she's here and regaled me with it the last few days. I hope she won't be disappointed, but I'm afraid she might. My mother probably won't be able to spend much time with her as she will be taking care of my father, at least when he gets released from the hospital.

My mother opens the door and breaks into a smile. She looks older than I remember her looking last time. There are more lines in her face and more grey streaks coloring her hair, but her eyes still twinkle the way they always have.

"Joy," she says and bends down with her arms out.

"Nana." Joy runs into her arms, squeezing the woman tightly about the neck. "You smell like cookies."

A smile plays across my lips. My mother always smelled of vanilla and sugar, and while she did often have a plate of cookies waiting for me when I arrived home from school, she didn't every day, and I often wondered how she still smelled of cookies on those days.

"That's because I have some in the kitchen." She taps the end of Joy's nose, earning a giggle. "Now, come in, and let's get you settled."

"Then can we have cookies?" Joy asks. She is bouncing up and down, sending the lights in her pink sneakers into overdrive. Mother nods, smiling at her enthusiasm.

I pull the two suitcases into the homey entrance and shut the door behind me.

The house hasn't changed a bit. A wooden coatrack still sits just to the right of the front door, holding Dad's derby cap and a few coats, and the sign, announcing "As for me and my house, we will serve the Lord," still hangs prominently on the wall. I shed my coat, adding it to the rack and then remove Joy's as well.

"Let me show you to your room." My mother grabs Joy's free hand and leads her down the beige carpeted hallway. Pictures of Anna and I line the walls. My mother never let an opportunity to take a picture go by, and I'm almost certain she bought every school picture we ever had so she could display them all on the walls. I tried to remove one once and replace it with something else, but she noticed right away and forced me to rehang that picture.

Mother opens the door to what was the guest room. Though it is still the guest room, she has added some decorations for a younger child to enjoy. The daybed has been covered with a flowery pink and purple bedspread and a blond doll is propped on top. An old dollhouse sits near the dresser along with a faded toy box filled with toys.

"This is all for me?" Joy's eyes are wide as she looks up at my mother.

The lines around my mother's eyes are more visible as she smiles. "Yep, all for you. A girl needs proper toys."

"Especially in this town," I say under my breath. Not quietly enough though as my mother shoots a look full of daggers my direction. How quickly she can change from sugar to fire. I hold my hand up in silent apology.

"Where is Daddy staying?"

"Right across the hall," my mother says, opening the door. My old room stares back at me, looking very much like it did in high school. My football awards still line the shelf, though they are coated in a fine layer of dust, and the tattered posters of my favorite bands cover the walls.

"Didn't feel like updating this one?" I ask.

My mother shrugs. "Maybe I would have if you came around more often."

I want to reply, but I don't want to start a fight, so I bite my tongue and carry the suitcase inside. After dropping off Joy's suitcase as well, we follow my mother back towards the open living room and into the country-themed kitchen. I've always hated the flowered wallpaper trim that circles the kitchen, but my mother hung it herself and has always loved it.

A plate of chocolate chip cookies sits in the middle of the scratched kitchen table. The usual wild flower display has been pushed to the side. Joy turns eager eyes on me.

"You may have one," I say, holding up a finger. "I don't want you to spoil your dinner."

She climbs up in a chair and snatches a cookie off the top of the pile, shoving most of it in her mouth.

I shake my head at her. "You could chew more slowly."

Her ravenous munching changes to a thoughtful chewing, and I join her at the table, plucking a cookie for myself off the pile.

"How is Dad?" I ask before taking a bite. My father is the whole reason I am here. He is in the hospital after falling off a ladder and fracturing his skull. Though my mother said I didn't need to come, I couldn't very well stay in Dallas if there was a chance this was life threatening, and brain bleeds often can be. Plus, she might need some help with him when he gets released. I doubt he'll be as active as he was before the accident. However, I am in the middle of a big presentation, one that could set me up for life with an even bigger company, so I left strict instructions with my assistant to keep me in the loop.

A flicker of doubt erases her twinkling for a moment before she recovers. "He is doing better today. The nurses say he only had a few instances of confusion yesterday, but they want to run another CT tomorrow."

"Any idea on when he'll be released?" I take a bite of the cookie, enjoying the warm chocolate goodness. I have missed my mom's cooking.

"Probably another few days, but it depends on what the scan shows. He has a pretty big brain bleed."

"Your brain can bleed?" Joy's head pops up, her eyes as wide as saucers.

My mother shoots me an apologetic look and without saying it, we agree to finish this discussion later when little ears are not present.

"Don't worry," I say, patting her arm. "The brain is amazing and can heal itself. When does Anna get in?" Anna, my younger sister, has been away at college studying to become a nurse.

"She has finals this week, so she's coming as soon as she finishes the last one. Oh, and guess who else is back in town?"

I raise my eyebrow at her; I've never been a fan of the guessing game.

"Presley Hays."

Presley Hays. The name knocks the wind out of me like a sucker punch. I haven't thought of her in years. In high school, Presley had been my best friend – the one person who had made this town bearable – but for some reason we had grown apart when Morgan entered the picture, and then one-day Presley had come over to tell me she was going to France to attend Le Cordon Bleu.

"The cupcake shop?" I say the words for myself, but my mother smiles and nods.

"Who's Presley?" Joy asks, looking from my mother to me.

"Just an old friend," I say. Just an old friend.

Chapter Two - Presley

As the last customer finishes their treat and waves goodbye, I lock the door and smile to myself. This may not have been my original dream, but I'm starting to really like it here. There's something about the small town feel that I have missed.

Grabbing the cleaning rag that hangs over the silver faucet of the big basin sink, I begin wiping down the glass table tops. There are only five tables; the room is rather small, but it's big enough for my needs. Each table boasts two white wrought iron chairs — the fancy ones with the decorative backs and padded seats. They had cost me a fortune, but they reminded me of Paris, so I couldn't pass them up.

I glance up at the Eiffel Tower. Trudy, the local artist painted it on one wall for me. It's not the same as when I could see it out my apartment window, but it's a close second, and she did it for a month's worth of treats. I'm certain I came out on top of that deal, and at least this view doesn't come with a cheating boyfriend.

My eyes narrow as I picture Pierre, the handsome Parisian I had been dating in Paris. He had seemed too good to be true and now I knew why. For all his good qualities, Pierre had the nasty habit of being unable to be faithful to one woman. When I had hinted I knew he was cheating, he hadn't even denied it. Instead, he had played it off like philandering was acceptable in France, and maybe it was, but it was unacceptable to me, so I had packed up my things and come home.

Star Lake, Texas was never my dream, but I'm not sure what my dream was before Brandon Scott walked into my life. The day I met him, my dream began to include Brandon and a five-star dessert shop in some upscale city, maybe even Paris. We used to talk for hours how we would get away from the small town and live life in a big city, but part of that dream had ended the day he told me Morgan was pregnant.

I had hoped she would be a leaf in the wind like all the rest of the women had been. Brandon never stayed with one woman for long, and he couldn't stay single between them for long either. It was obvious he was looking for something and not finding it. I had always hoped it was because he was looking for me, but Morgan had been different.

She had been exotic and wealthy, vacationing for the summer to get away from her busy city life. With her beautiful dark hair and stunning blue eyes, she had hooked him from the beginning, and they had been inseparable. I had lost my best friend that summer long before I left town.

I should have told him how I felt before she came along, but I had been too afraid, and I'd always thought I'd have a little more time.

An incessant rapping at the front door breaks my reminiscing, and I look up to see Trudy frantically waving from the other side.

This had better be good. She knows I close at six.

"You'll never guess what I just heard." Her excitement is punctuated by the squealing of her voice. Her trademark overalls are covered in paint splotches and a few random splatters dot her face and outer coat as well. A red bandanna covers up her dark hair. She must have been painting recently, though it is too dark for her to have been painting outside.

"What?" I ask, though I'm not very curious. In Star Lake, people get excited if Max puts a new dish on the menu. Well, some get excited. The old, crotchety people complain that the menu isn't the same, and they can't find their favorites.

"Paula said she saw new blood come into town today. A hottie."

I take this with a grain of salt. For one thing, Paula is the town's gossip, and if she doesn't have truthful tidbits, she tends to make them up just to have something to share. For another, Paula is in her forties, but still dresses like she's twenty in tight skirts and cleavage baring tops. She is so man hungry that she thinks anything male on two legs is a hottie. She once tried to date the preacher who must be close to seventy.

"Well, then good for Paula.".

Trudy shakes her head. "No, Paula said he was young. Like your age."

Trudy isn't much older than me, but she has decided she is too artistic for men. She doesn't want to be tied down with a relationship or a man wanting her attention when she wants to be painting.

"Then I'm sure I will meet him eventually." I'm not taking her bait. Ever since I returned a few months ago, the town has been trying to set me up with the few remaining single men I'm not related to. It's not a big town, so that has consisted of Justin, the recent high school graduate who bags groceries at the general store and hasn't decided what he wants to do with his life yet, Bert, the odd mail carrier who is single for very good reason – the man tried to establish a chicken petting farm for the elderly, and of course the seventy-year-old preacher. Most of the other people Brandon and I went to school with either moved away like we did or stayed but got married. Star Lake is great for families, but it is not a hopping singles spot.

"You're hopeless," she says, but she helps me turn the chairs over on the tabletops, so I can sweep the floor. "You need to get back out there."

"What do you want me to do?" I ask, grabbing the broom from behind the counter, "Camp on a rooftop with a pair of binoculars scanning for this hottie? It's a small town. If he does exist" – I emphasize the word does, drawing it out to two syllables to make my skepticism unmistakable – "then he'll come in here sooner or later."

She sticks her tongue out at me, but drops the subject and continues turning over chairs.

Though I'm not looking for a relationship after the disaster with Pierre, I can't help thinking that a man wouldn't be a terrible thing to have around. The limited dating pool is the one thing I don't like about this small town.

After the floor is swept, Trudy ducks out – citing the need to finish her masterpiece, but really it's because she doesn't like menial work, and I take the remaining pastries out of the display case and wrap them up. They can only keep for another day, but I'm hopeful they'll sell tomorrow. Business hasn't been booming since I started, more like a steady trickle, but it's been good enough to keep the lights on so far. However, if something doesn't change soon, I may have to close the doors, and I have no idea what I'll do then.

Sparing one final glance to make sure it's tidy, I don my coat and hat. The December air has chilled considerably the last few days, and by the time I leave at night, it's almost always near freezing. The first snow must be right around the corner. Shoving my hands in my pocket, I begin the walk home.

My breath creates tiny wisps of smoke as I exhale, and the tip of my nose grows cold. I'm glad I don't live far from the shop. Glancing down Cooper street as I pass, I can just make out Brandon's parent's house.

I don't know why I bother to look when I know he isn't there, but it's a gesture I can't seem to stop. Maybe it's from so many times of looking down the street when we were younger. The few times we snuck out, we would meet on this street corner before driving to nearby Mesa for a party, and every time after leaving his house, I would stop here and turn back, hoping to find him running after me to sweep me up in a kiss.

I've heard his father is still in the hospital after his fall, and I wonder if Anna will come back to see him. I know Brandon won't, as the last I heard, he hasn't been home since moving away. Probably too busy with his business and his family.

Unbidden, thoughts of Brandon fill my head, and I wonder about his kid. Is it a boy who looks like him or a girl with the beauty of Morgan? The child would be about five now, possibly even in Kindergarten. I picture him sitting with the child at a table and doing homework. In my mind, it is always a girl with Morgan's eyes who will hold a piece of Brandon's heart that no other woman will ever touch.

Shaking my head to clear the traitorous thoughts, I continue walking. Though I haven't spoken with his mother recently, I decide to bake the family something special to let them know I'm thinking about them. After all, for years they were a second family to me.

Half a block later, I reach my apartment. It's actually a mother-in-law suite attached to my mother's house, but as it has its own entrance. I like to call it my own apartment, and my mother works so much that I rarely see her anyway. Entering, I toss my coat on the rack before calling for my cat, Niko.

He really is the perfect man – considerate, always happy to see me, and shares my bed without taking it over. If only he were a man and not a cat. He climbs up on my lap as I sit on the couch and flick on the TV. The images flash in front of my eyes, but my mind is on the hottie. Whether he lives up to his title or not, I'm curious as to who he is and why he's here.

Our big tourist season is usually in the summer, when rich families from the city decide to test out a rustic life for a few weeks, though a small handful do come in the winter as we typically get at least one good snowfall. Maybe he's a food critic who's heard about my shop and come to taste the wares. Smiling at the thought, I allow myself to be sucked into the dream.

Chapter Three - Brandon

"So, it's true. The prodigal son has returned."

Dropping my fork, I turn to my sister, who is staring at me, a bag still slung over her shoulder. She must have just gotten in. Her blond hair, so unlike my darker shade, skims her thin shoulders. All our lives people have wondered how we are related as she inherited my mother's pale skin and blond hair while I got our father's darker Italian skin and hair.

"Hey Anna." I cross to her and envelop her in a hug. She is taller and thinner, and a flicker of regret at the years I haven't seen her rises inside me. When we first moved to Star Lake, the two of us had joined forces in trying to convince our parents to move back. It was only after meeting Presley that Anna and I started to grow apart.

"How long are you staying?" She drops her bag and grabs a plate from the cupboard, joining me at the table. Her fork stabs three pancakes, and she douses them in Maple syrup before taking a giant bite. She is either not eating at college or has taken up a grueling exercise regimen to be able to eat like that and stay thin.

"Until Dad is better, but I'm in the middle of a huge presentation deal right now, so I'll have to get back soon."

"Look who I found," my mother says entering the kitchen with Joy attached to her hand.

"Morning, Bug." I open my arms, and she runs into them.

"Who are you?" she asks when she notices Anna.

"This is my sister Anna. She's your aunt." Due to school, Anna had only come with my parent's once, so Joy hasn't seen her as often.

"Aunt Anna?" Her nose wrinkles, and she shakes her head. "That doesn't sound right. I'll just call you Auntie Anne, like the pretzels. Can we have a pretzel Daddy?"

"Not right now," I say, depositing her into her own chair. "Right now, it's breakfast time, and your grandmother made pancakes, but maybe we can go into town later and check out the new bakery."

"The bakery or the baker?" Anna asks between bites of pancake, a teasing glint evident in her eye.

I shoot her a warning glare while placing a few pancakes on Joy's plate, but wonder at the question myself. I haven't seen or spoken with Presley in over five years, so why I am so curious about her now?

After breakfast, we load into the car to drive the few miles to the hospital. It sits just outside of town, and unlike Star Lake, it is state of the art. In fact, most of the towns near ours are more up to date. It's like our town got stuck in a time warp or something.

Mother always said it was because the leaders of Star Lake enjoyed the slower pace of life in a small town, but it baffled me how anyone could enjoy our town. Or maybe I am disillusioned because once I thought of settling down in this town, until Morgan left.

My throat begins to close as we pull into the parking lot. I haven't been in this hospital since Joy was born, and while that was a happy event, it relates to Morgan leaving, which was not. Thankfully, Mom and Anna are here with me.

My mother offers to take Joy to the family waiting room as we enter the hospital. The look on her face tells me my father is evidently still bruised up. I mentally prepare myself for what I'll see, but I am still shocked when we enter the room. His left eye is swollen shut and colored a bright purple. There is a monitor hooked to his finger, and an IV pumping fluids in his arm. He hears us enter and opens his good eye.

"Brandon? Is that you?" His voice is clear, which gives me hope that he is better than he looks. I'm not sure if it's his injuries or the hospital bed itself, but he appears old and frail as he lays beneath the white sheets. I bat away another ping of regret. Even if I lived closer, I couldn't keep my parents from aging or falling off ladders.

"Hi Dad. Anna's here too."

She steps around from behind me and crosses to the other side of his bed. "Hi Daddy. You look awful." The words are her defense mechanism. Fear is evident in her eyes as she grabs his hand and holds it tight.

A labored laugh escapes his mouth before he grimaces in pain and grabs his stomach. "Sorry, broken ribs."

"What were you thinking Dad?"

His one good eye focuses on me. "I guess I wasn't. I thought I was standing on something sturdy until I tumbled off it."

Anna's sniffle grabs both of our attention.

"Don't worry, honey, I'm going to be fine."

She nods, but a few more silent tears snake their way down her cheek.

"Joy is here too, and I'll bring her to see you, but I'll need to explain your face first," I say.

"And Morgan?"

My father has never given up hope that Morgan and I will get back together. Though he wasn't a fan of hers in the beginning, he is a strong believer that a home consists of two parents.

"Morgan's not coming back, Dad. She's moved on to bigger things."

In truth, I have no idea what Morgan is doing. We haven't heard from her since the day she walked out. She has sent no cards, no gifts, nothing. It's like she has erased us from her memory completely.

"I'll keep praying," he says.

I'm about to tell him he can keep his prayers for himself when a nurse walks in and says she needs to take him away for more tests. We each lean down to give him a hug and then watch as he is wheeled out of the room.

"Do you think he's okay?" Anna wipes the last tear from her cheek. She's always been the more emotional of the two of us.

I wrap my arm around her shoulders. "Yeah, he looked strong though bruised, and his speech sounded okay to me." Mother had told me last night they were keeping him for observation because his brain bleed wouldn't stop. They were hopeful it would clear up on its own after a few days because the other option involved drilling a hole in his skull.

After stopping at the nurse's station for directions, we continue down the hall to find Joy and Mother. Neither of us speaks, and I'm certain we are both entertaining the thought of what we will do if Dad doesn't come home. It's a sobering thought, and not one I want to dwell on very long.

The playroom isn't very big, but it has a small play structure, a few old computers, and a table with puzzles, which is where Joy is parked. I smile, watching her. The girl has loved puzzles since she was three. Often, I would realize how silent the house was and go searching for her only to find her at a table in her room turning pieces and sticking them in formation. At almost six, she is now working five hundred-piece puzzles.

"That was short," my mother says when she sees us.

"They took him for more tests. How was Joy?"

My mother smiles and points. "She's been there since we got here."

"Hey, Bug, you want to go get that pretzel now?"

Her head pops up, but there is indecision in her eyes. She bites her bottom lip, her telltale sign of concentration as she tries to decide between the puzzle and a pretzel. Food wins in the end, and she places the piece in her hand back on the table. That is definitely a trait she got from me. Morgan hardly ever touched food, but that's probably how she stayed so thin.

I make a mental note to check the general store for a puzzle for her. There isn't much to do in this town, and at least that will keep her busy when I need to be working.

I park the car in front of Max's, and we file out. "It is still okay to park here, right?" Max had always lived above his diner, and though he has an old beat up truck, he had always parked it in the alley.

My mother nods. "Yes, Max hasn't changed much, though I hear he's seeing someone now."

"Who?" Anna asks. I could have cared less about any town gossip, but Anna ate it up. She had always liked to be in the know. "Oh, please tell me it's Layla. I'll just die if it's anyone else."

"It is indeed Layla. They finally got together after she almost married Mr. Jones, remember him?"

"Daddy, can we go see if they have pretzels now?" Joy is tugging on my pant leg and eagerly pointing to the shop across the street. I'm glad for the distraction and the ability to focus on something other than Max's love life.

After checking both directions for traffic, though there almost never is any, I let her scurry across the street. "I'll be right behind you. As soon as these two yentas stop yakking."

My sister punches my arm, but they follow Joy across the street.

"I'll be right there. I'm just going to check the store for something." Hurrying to the general store, I hope not to run into anyone. It's not that I don't like the people of this town, but when you've been gone for a while, everyone wants to hear your entire life story, and I just don't feel like sharing right now.

Chapter Four –
Presley

The silver bell above the door announces visitors, and I look up to see a small girl with dark curls enter. Her coat and shoes are the same color of pink, and her shoes light up as she crosses the floor. I'm terrible at judging ages, but I guess the girl to be five or six. She carries an air of confidence for her young age as she sidles up to the dessert case.

"Well, hello there. What can I get for you?" Placing my arms on the top of the counter, I smile down at her.

She scans the offerings, her index finger tapping against her pink lips, before glancing up at me. "Do you have pretzels?"

I see her mouth move, but the words barely register as my focus is on her eyes. Those eyes are blazoned in my memory, the eyes of the woman who stole my love – although granted she didn't know he was my love. Could I be looking into the eyes of his child?

My questions are confirmed a moment later when his mother, Beverly, and his sister enter my shop. Though I've seen Beverly a time or two around town since returning, this is the first time I've spoken with her or with Anna since I left.

"Hello, Presley." Beverly's voice is nice and calm. She hadn't always been that way, but once she had mellowed out, her calm demeanor had been one of my favorite things about Brandon's family. My own mother was always rushed and hectic, but it's because she had to be, working two jobs to support Ryan and I after Dad left.

Beverly, on the other hand, had never had to work. Her husband, Bruce, had owned a software company, and when he retired, they had moved here to Star Lake. When we first met, she had still been uptight and obsessed with money, but a few months of this town wears anyone down, and by her first Christmas here, she was wearing jeans and sweaters instead of business suits and pearls.

"Hello Beverly, Anna." I nod my head at each of them. Anna looks grown up, with her hair down around her shoulders instead of always in a ponytail the way she wore it in High School. She's also thinner, and her face has taken on a more womanly, angular shape. She's only a few years younger than Brandon and me, but when you are sixteen and seventeen, those few years of maturity matter. Now, I imagine we would be close friends, if we didn't have the giant elephant of Brandon between us.

The little girl, young as she is, is smart. Her eyes travel from her family to me and back again. Though she may not understand everything, she catches on that something is amiss.

"What did you want again, honey?" I hope it is something in the back I must go look for. My guess is that if his daughter is here, then Brandon is too, unless he and Morgan shipped her off to have some time alone. Regardless, I want to check my appearance in case he or she enter my store.

Her words, "a pretzel," fill me with relief. I don't have any of those in the front counter, but there are a few frozen in the freezer.

"I have some in the back. Would you like one as well?" I ask Beverly and Anna.

"Not for me," Anna says. "I'll have one of those." She points to a chocolate éclair on the bottom shelf.

"That looks delicious. I'll have one too," Beverly agrees.

"Wonderful, I'll be right back."

The freezer is at the back of the shop, but just across from it is the bathroom. I duck into the tiny room first and cringe at the face in the mirror. My hair is piled in a messy pony; the purple streak hanging loose near my face, and a smudge of white flour resides on one cheek. Wiping at the smudge, I push the loose hair back behind my ear. It is not a perfect look, but it's the best I can do for now.

Darting into the freezer and grabbing the pretzel, I unwrap it as I head to the toaster oven. In it goes, and I set the timer for two minutes, just enough to warm it without making it hard and chewy. When it dings, I wrap it in some wax paper and take it back out to the girl.

A smile lights up her face, and she chomps on the pastry. Suppressing my laughter, I extract two chocolate eclairs and hold them out to the women. Beverly hands me a twenty, and I am making change when the bill jingles again.

A shudder runs down my spine, and I know who it is before even looking up. I hand the change to Beverly, but my eyes are not on her. They are on the man with the chocolate brown eyes and the full beard. He looks older with the beard. Masculinity rolls off him in invisible waves, but I am the only one affected.

His eyes catch mine, and just like that I fall again. There's something about those intoxicating brown eyes that have always sucked me in. The day we met flashes in my mind.

"What are you drawing?"

The voice over my shoulder startles me, and I slam the sketchpad closed. I don't share my drawings with anyone. They aren't very good, just one of my ways to escape reality. The other is baking, but I can't do that at school. "Are you talking to me?"

He swings his lean frame onto the bench next to me, and the smell of him floats on the air. Soap and sandalwood. I lift my eyes to his face. Liquid pools of chocolate grip my gaze, and my heart stops in my chest.

"I don't see anyone else drawing around here, do you?" His eyes twinkle as if he's teasing me, but why would he do that? He doesn't even know me.

What is he doing talking to me? Doesn't he know he should be hanging with the other rich kids, and not with me? "But why are you talking to me?" I tuck my purple streak behind my ear and try not to turn the shade of red I feel inside, but the heat of my ears tells me I am losing that battle.

"Well, I thought you seemed interesting, and you were sitting over here all by yourself. I'm Brandon by the way." He sticks out his hand, and I stare at it, afraid to shake it. What if my hand is sweaty? What if I have paint or charcoal on my fingers? I don't usually care about those things, but this is Brandon Scott, hottie new arrival to town and every girl's dream.

"I know who you are." My eyes drop back down to the sketchpad in my lap. "Everyone knows who Brandon Scott is."

"Hey, Presley." He says the words as if it's only been days since we've seen each other and not six years. "You look good." His voice is deep and rich, different than when we were in high school and yet still the same.

"Hi Brandon. It's been a while." I want to slap my forehead. Six years I've dreamed of this moment, and that's all I can say? Where are all the flowery words I practiced over and over in my head for the time I saw him next?

A smile tugs on his lips, and I know he knows I'm uncomfortable. He's always been able to read me like an open book, which I used to love, but now I wish he'd slam the cover closed and put the book back on the shelf. We don't have that relationship anymore. He doesn't deserve to be able to read me.

"I see you've met my daughter, Joy."

My eyes flutter to the girl, who has nearly finished her pretzel. Joy is a pretty name, and it suits her. It is easy to imagine that she brings joy to those around her with her mesmerizing eyes and Brandon's contagious smile. As the women get up from a table, I realize that Beverly and Anna had moved away and seated themselves. I have no idea when.

"She seems lovely." Though I mean the words, they sound forced and trite as they come out. "Would you like a pastry too?"

He smiles at me, and the world goes silent. The surrounding noises and shapes fade away, and it is just him and me. "Of course," he says. He points to one of my double chocolate espresso brownies, and on autopilot, I take it out of the case and hand it to him.

I don't even remember to charge him, but he smiles and places a five next to the register for me. "It was good to see you," he says, and then the four of them walk out of my shop. The little girl turns and waves, breaking the spell.

When they are out of sight, I sink to the floor. My heart is racing as if I've just downed five cups of coffee. I place a hand over it to slow the beating. I had thought I was over Brandon, but I was clearly just denying my feelings.

Chapter Five - Brandon

As the door closes behind us, I can't help but sneak one final glance at Presley. She had always been beautiful, though she didn't know it, but age has defined her features even more. Her face has shed the extra roundness from childhood, accentuating her soft cheekbones and the slender curve of her neck. Her eyes are still the same arresting blue they had been back in high school, the kind that is hard to look away from. It was her eyes that first drew me to her.

When I had arrived in Star Lake as a Sophomore, I had known no one, and was angry at leaving my friends behind. My father's money had attracted people, but none I had wanted to call friends, but when I saw the quiet blond girl across the way in the lunchroom, I felt drawn to see what she was all about.

"What are you drawing?" I lean over her shoulder to try and get a glimpse of her sketch pad. She always has it with her, and I am curious what she draws in it. She rarely speaks though we have several classes together.

She tucks the purple strand of hair behind her ear that always falls in her face and looks up with piercing blue eyes that cause my heartbeat to speed up in my chest. They are beautiful and breathtaking. "Are you talking to me?"

I swing my lean frame onto the bench next to her and turn on my charm. "I don't see anyone else drawing around here, do you?"

She stares at me, unaffected. "But why are you talking to me?"

I blink, unaccustomed to my charm not working. "Well, I thought you seemed interesting, and you were sitting over here all by yourself. I'm Brandon by the way." I stick out my hand, and she looks at it but doesn't take the offer.

"I know who you are." She drops her attention back down to her sketchpad. "Everyone knows who Brandon Scott is."

That had been the beginning of my interest in her. I wasn't used to someone who didn't fall at my feet right away, and at first it had been about the challenge. I had wanted to get her to open up to me, but the more I'd gotten to know her, the more I realized she was an amazing person who completed me in a way I didn't understand.

Though quiet in large groups, she was fiercely opinionated in private, and she always called me out on my crap, which no one had ever done before. Her calm and quirky manner had also soothed my irritation at being in this new town, and our friendship had grown.

At some point, I had fallen in love with her, but was too afraid to tell her. Too afraid to lose my best friend and my link to sanity in this tiny town. So, I had buried my feelings and sought comfort in the arms of other girls, but none of them made me feel the way I did when I was with Presley, at least not until Morgan came along.

"Daddy, let's go." Joy tugs on my hand, pulling my thoughts back into the present. "I want to see the ducks."

"Yeah, Romeo. Get your head out of the clouds and join us." Anna's eyes twinkle as she teases me.

I flash her another warning glare. There is no time for romance; I'm only here until our father gets a little better, and then it's back to the city and my job. Still, it would be nice to see Presley again, just to catch up on old times.

I allow myself to be drug down the sidewalk and try to see the town from Joy's eyes.

"Look, an ice cream shop." Her little finger jabs to the right. "Can we go sometime, Daddy?"

If it hasn't changed, Mr. Perkins runs the ice cream shop. It used to be one of our favorite hangouts. Presley and I would often stop in after school and sit on the red padded barstools and order milkshakes, making faces at each other in the large mirror that hung on the wall behind the counter.

"Sure, we can," but she is already pointing at the old dollar cinema, which still appears to be playing movies and then at Ms. Paula's dance studio. I'm relieved as the shops of downtown fade, and we reach the more residential part of town.

The trees have all lost their leaves for the winter; the remnants of them crunch under our feet. A cool breeze blows a few tattered pieces across the sidewalk and lifts strands of Joy's hair.

"There it is." Her voice is shrill with excitement as she drops my hand and runs to the lake. It hasn't iced over yet, but it will with the first big snow. Star Lake never has a long winter, but it generally has at least one or two good snows between December and February.

The few ducks on the lake scatter as Joy runs at them, sending her into gales of laughter. As they fly off, she runs after them. If nothing else, she will expend some energy here.

"She looks happy," my mother says, placing a hand on my arm.

"She's happy in Dallas."

"Is she?"

My mother leaves it at that, but her damage is done. Watching Joy running after the ducks and tossing rocks into the lake, I wonder if she is happy in Dallas. Due to my work schedule, she is usually taken to school by our nanny, Amber, who drops her off on her way to her own college classes. Then Amber picks her up from school and stays with her until I get home around six or seven in the evening. Joy and I then have dinner and play for an hour or two before it's time for bed.

The thought plagues me the remainder of the time we are at the park and on the walk back to the car. I decide to make the most of this trip. There may not be another chance like this to hang out with Joy if the proposal I'm working on gets accepted.

Chapter Six - Presley

"So, the hottie is Brandon Scott?" Trudy asks before shoving a fry in her mouth. We are eating a late dinner at The Diner.

I drop my head in my hands. "Yes, and I thought I was over him, but I am clearly not."

"Why don't you just tell him how you feel," Max says as he places a hamburger and fries in front of me. His ballcap is turned around on his head in his signature style, and his plaid today is a blue and white. We are not close, but Max has a habit of listening to conversations and butting in with his advice whether it is asked for or not.

"Because I don't know if Morgan's still in the picture for one," I say, rattling the reasons off on my sparkly painted fingers. I should give up my glitter nail polish now that I'm in my late twenties, but like my purple streak it has been a part of me for so long, I'm not sure I can part with it. "He lives hours away from here for another, and I don't even know if he likes me. What if he's never thought of me as more than a friend?"

"Seems to me since you aren't really friends anymore that it wouldn't matter."

Before I can respond, he whirls around and returns to the kitchen, but I hear him mutter "women" as the door closes behind him.

"You know, he might be right," Trudy says. "You haven't spoken to him in years, so it's not like you'd be losing anything."

Except my fantasies. I'm ashamed to admit that part of my fear is hearing him say he's never thought of me as more than a friend and no longer having hope to cling to.

"Here's an idea. Why don't you take him and his daughter to the holiday fair this weekend? Layla is going to have a pie tasting competition and Bert is planning to make candles. If nothing else, it will be some cheap entertainment."

I roll the thought over in my head as I take a bite of the burger. It would be fun to spend more time with him and at least catch up on old times, that is if Morgan isn't in the picture.

The next day, gathering my courage, I pack a basket of pastries for the family. I'd been planning to bring them over anyway, but realize now they will make a great excuse if Morgan is around. After donning my coat and locking the shop, I force my feet to follow the once often walked path to Brandon's parents' house.

The yellow house is just as I remember it, if not a little more worn. The porch step creaks under my footstep, and I cringe at the sound. I should have remembered that step. It was what got us caught one night when we came home after curfew. The image of his mother, irate and red, brings a smile to my face. If only we'd been doing something worth getting so worked up over instead of innocently studying for a test at my place and simply losing track of time. I almost lose my nerve and turn back, but my finger touches the doorbell before I can retreat.

Anna opens the door and smiles at me. There is knowledge in her smile. She is not fooled by my ruse of freshly baked goods.

"Come in." She opens the door wider, and I shuffle inside, ducking my head to hide the pink flag across my cheeks. "Brandon and Mother are in the family room." She begins to lead the way, but my hand reaches out to stay her arm. Curious, she turns back to me.

"Anna, is . . ." I don't really know how to ask what is on my mind, but I can't go in there without knowing. "Is Morgan out of the picture?" I spit the words out before I can change my mind about asking them. Waiting to hear my fate, my hands grip the basket tighter. Her eyes twinkle, and she nods. Relief floods my body so quickly that my knees buckle. She grabs my elbow before I tumble to the floor, and I thank her with my eyes. When my legs regain their strength, she resumes her walk to the family room.

I feel him before I see him. His presence is like a giant magnet, drawing me to him. He looks up from his phone as I enter.

"Presley? What are you doing here?"

My ears flame, and I'm glad my hair is long enough to cover them. "I heard about your father, and I wanted to bring you some pastries. It isn't much, but . . ."

"It is wonderful, my dear. Thank you." Beverly stands and takes the basket, exiting the room and pulling Anna behind her. I'm left alone with Brandon, who looks as uncomfortable as I feel.

"Here, sit," he says finally, pointing to an empty space on the couch next to him.

Despite being afraid to sit next to him, afraid to be too close to his magnetic pull, my feet propel me there anyway. "It was good to see you yesterday."

"Yes, you too."

There is an electricity running between us. I can hear the soft buzz of it, and the hair on my arms is standing up. I'm drowning in those dark pools once again.

"How was Paris?"

The breathiness of his voice tells me he is feeling something similar. Could it be that he has feelings for me as well?

My tongue swipes my bottom lip, and his eyes follow the movement before returning to mine. "It was nice, until it wasn't. I met a guy there, but it . . . it didn't work out."

His hand grabs mine. "Presley, I'm sorry to hear that."

A fiery tingle runs up my arm at his touch, and my eyes drop to our entwined fingers. My throat has gone dry, and it is hard to form my next words. "I'm sorry about Morgan." I pull my gaze up as I finish the words to judge his expression.

His posture stiffens, and his eyes harden for just a second before returning to their normal soft gaze. "It was unfortunate, but I'd rather her be gone than stay and not be the mother Joy needs."

Though a beard coats most of his face, his lips are still visible, and my gaze can't help but fall to them. They are thin, pink, and perfect. "Um, so there's a festival tomorrow. I thought maybe you and Joy would like to go with me?" My breath catches at the last word and holds.

The twinkle that haunts my dreams lights his eyes, and he squeezes my hand. "I'd love that, as will Joy. What time is it?"

Relief washes over me, and the breath releases. "It starts at noon and runs all afternoon, so I'll meet you here at 11:30 and we can walk in together."

"Great. I'm sure Joy will be excited." He tucks his phone in his jeans and stares back at me.

Another silence stretches out between us. I hate that we are reduced to small talk. I miss my friend I could tell anything. "Okay, well, I should be going. It's getting late, and you probably want to get some sleep." Not wanting to, I rise from the couch, which separates our hands. They cry out at the missing warmth, but I refrain from reaching for him.

A look crosses his face. I'm not sure if its disappointment or if I just want it to be. "Let me walk you home then."

"Oh, you don't have to do that. It's not far."

A genuine smile lights his face. "I know it's not far. I used to walk there every day, remember?"

I remember. How could I forget? It was generally the highlight of my day. "If you want, but you don't have to."

"I want," he says, and for a moment I see the old Brandon, the teasing twinkle in his eyes and his trademark lopsided smile.

I follow him to the front door, where he grabs his coat and scarf. The winter air slaps our faces as we step out on the front porch. Pulling my coat tighter, I sink deeper in it to keep the heat locked inside.

"Are you cold?" He unwraps his scarf and holds it out to me. It isn't quite the gesture I was hoping for, but I accept and wrap it around my neck, enjoying the little bit of warmth it adds and the scent of Brandon that now fills my nose.

The stars are out, reminding me of the many times we laid in the back of his pickup bed and watched them. I've forgotten how bright they are here with few lights blocking their shine. "They're so beautiful."

"What?"

"The stars." I point to the sky. "I never saw them this bright in Paris. Too many lights."

His eyes follow my hands, and he pauses. I stop beside him. "Do you remember the time our Senior year we fell asleep in the truck after watching the stars?"

My ears begin their slow burn again. I have been replaying the exact memory in my head. He fell asleep before I did that night, and I could have woken him, but instead I curled against his chest, enjoying the beating of his heart in my ear and the steady rise and fall of his muscular chest under my hand. "Mother was so mad when I came in the next morning. She didn't believe me that we didn't do anything but sleep."

"Mine either." His laugh is as I remember it, deep and melodious, and it elicits a laugh from me in return. "Maybe we should do it again."

"We would freeze," I say, punching his arm. "We'll have to wait until summer when it warms up."

Immediately I regret the words as his smile fades. "Right, summer. I'll be gone by then. Back to the city."

I curse my bad timing. I've ruined the mood. We continue the walk. "How long are you staying?" I don't want to hear the answer, but my heart needs to. It needs to be reminded that whatever it is feeling now, it cannot last. Brandon will go home in a few weeks, leaving me alone again.

He shrugs. "I'm not sure. A week, maybe two. Until my father is released and then probably a few more days to make sure Mother can take care of him."

It is as I expected, not near enough time or too much, depending on how you look at it. We finish the walk in silence.

At my door, I stop and turn to him. "Thank you for the walk." There is so much more I want to say, but the words won't form the way I want them to.

His eyes stare into mine, and I wonder if he is having the same problem. He takes another step toward me, closing the distance, and his hands grab mine again. His fingers are cold, but I don't care. The heat between the two of us is slowly warming us both.

"It really is good to see you, Presley. I didn't know it, but I've missed our friendship."

The word is like an icy dagger to my heart. Friends. I force a tight smile. "Me too."

His eyes linger a moment longer, and I think maybe, just maybe, there's something more than friendship in them. Maybe he'll lean across the few inches separating us and place his lips on mine. My hand fights the urge to reach up and touch his beard. I want to feel it, to see if it is soft like his hair. I swallow as I hold his gaze, and then it's gone.

He clears his throat and releases my hands. "I'll see you tomorrow."

"Good night."

Though the air is still cold, I stand and watch him as he walks away.

Chapter Seven - Presley

My eyes open before the alarm goes off. I'm not much for sleeping in on the weekends anyway, but the thought of spending the day with Brandon kept me up half the night. I should be tired, but a stream of adrenaline courses through me. Still, I know this high won't last, so after dressing, I start a pot of coffee.

Niko finds my lap as I curl up with the steaming beverage. His back arches against my free hand, begging to be petted. As I stroke his black and white fur, his purr reverberates against my leg, and his paws knead my jeans. Thankfully whoever owned him before had him declawed.

A week after I moved back to town, Niko had shown up on my doorstep. It was like he knew I was lonely. I'd asked around town as he looked well cared for, but no one could remember seeing him before. That had been my sign I was supposed to keep him.

"What am I doing, Niko? I shouldn't be falling for him again. His life isn't here. This is only going to end in heartbreak again." Niko says nothing, which is another thing I love about him. He's the only man who's ever been in my life who just listens.

When the coffee is finished, I rinse the cup in the sink, place it on the small counter, and check my appearance in the hall mirror one final time. I'm no Morgan, but my hair has actually agreed to hold a curl today, and it falls gently on my shoulders. My tiny bit of eye makeup accentuates the intensity of my blue eyes, and my lips even have a sparkly sheen. Not bad.

Though late morning, the air is still chilly, and I shiver inside my coat. By the time I reach Brandon's, my fingers are nearly numb. Hopefully most of this festival is going to be indoors, or we won't be able to stay long.

I step over the creaky third step this time and place my finger on the small ornate doorbell and wait, my heart pumping loudly in my chest. I hope Brandon won't be able to hear the sound.

The melodic chime echoes through the door, and it swings open, revealing Brandon still in sweats. His disheveled hair gives the appearance of just crawling out of bed. I glance at my watch. It's past eleven thirty am.

"Did you just wake up?" I ask not bothering to hide the incredulity in my voice.

"Hello to you too," he says and runs his hand across his beard. "I slept in later than normal. It must be from traveling."

My eyebrows raise. I don't know where he's living now, but I had thought it was still in Texas. "Okay, well are you still up for the festival?"

He nods and opens the door wider. "Joy has been talking about it non-stop, so even if I weren't, I have to be." His lopsided grin reflects how much love he has for his daughter. "Go on into the kitchen. I'll clean up and meet you there."

My eyes linger on his face a moment longer, and I look away when the thought of him in the shower begins to heat my cheeks.

Oblivious, he turns and walks down the hallway, and I continue into the kitchen. Beverly and Joy are at the table, coloring in old coloring books.

"Good morning, Presley," Beverly says, looking up from the book. "Would you like to join us?"

I try to conceal the smile tugging at my lips. Coloring has long been a favorite pastime of mine. I pull out the chair next to Joy and pick up one of the other books on the table. It's an old one of princesses. Flipping through the pages to find a clean one, I glance over at Joy. Her face is focused on her coloring, and she reminds me very much of Brandon whenever he was studying for a test. She has the same habit of scrunching her nose and occasionally sticking her tongue out of the corner of her mouth.

"So, Joy, are you excited about the festival today?" I ask reaching for a light blue crayon.

Her crayon pauses, and she looks up at me, eyes sparkling with delight. "I am so excited. I have been thinking about it all night. Nana says there's a pie tasting and hot chocolate and popcorn stringing. I've never strung popcorn." Her words tumble out like a waterfall.

"There's that and a whole lot more. When I was young there were lots of ornament decorating tables. Those were always my favorite."

"That sounds fun." Then her face clouds over. "Course we don't usually put ornaments on the tree because Daddy is too busy."

I look to Beverly who shrugs. Somehow, I cannot imagine Brandon not celebrating Christmas. It was always our favorite holiday.

The first Christmas we spent together, he snuck me into the forest just outside of town and we wandered through the trees for hours until we found the perfect one. He whipped out a saw and cut down a Virginia pine. It wasn't quite the same as the pine trees he was used to in Washington, but it was a close second. We drug the tree back through the forest, losing a lot of the needles in the process, loaded it into his truck bed, and drove it to his house.

Once there, we turned on some Christmas music and unloaded the box of ornaments his family had brought with them. Hours later, we had lain under the tree and stared up at the lights, exhausted and proud. I can't imagine the man who did all that with me no longer excited about Christmas.

"You mean he doesn't decorate a tree with you?"

"He doesn't usually even remember a tree until the last few days." Her voice takes on a melancholic tone as she turns back to her coloring. "Then we go to whatever local store still has some and get whatever is still there. Sometimes Amber helps me decorate, but Daddy doesn't have much, so the tree still always looks sad."

"Like a Charlie Brown tree?"

"Who's Charlie Brown?"

"Never mind," I say, shaking my head.

As she shrugs her tiny shoulders in defeat, I make a mental promise to remind Brandon of the fun we used to have here. Whatever Morgan and living in a big city has done to him, my hope is that it can be cured with a little small-town magic.

My crayon moves across the picture adding shading and depth to the gown the long-haired girl is wearing, but my mind is a million miles away thinking about how best to reconnect Brandon with the roots he seems to have forgotten.

"Are we going to sit around and color all day?"

His voice startles me, and the crayon jumps in my hand, sending a blue line outside of the dress and across the girl's arm. A small sigh of frustration escapes my lips. It is just a silly book, but as an artist, I take pride in my work, and now this piece is ruined.

Joy slams her book closed with such force that the crayons bounce on the table. "Yes, let's go."

"You better dress warm. It was quite cold on the way here," I say, carefully closing my book and stacking it back in the middle. "Beverly, are you coming with us?"

"Of course, I wouldn't miss it for the world," his mother says, closing her own book and putting the crayons away in the box.

"What about Anna?" My preoccupation with Brandon has kept me from noticing Anna's absence until now.

"She's still sleeping," Beverly replies, "but I'll leave her a note to tell her where we've gone. I can't stay too long though. I need to get out to see Bruce today."

"How is he doing?" I ask as we moved to the living room to grab coats. Joy is already in hers and tugging on Brandon's sleeve in excitement.

"Better. They think he'll get to come home soon, but he won't be able to drive for at least a month."

"Good thing there's nowhere to drive around here." Brandon's words are followed by a snort, another new and unattractive habit he has picked up since the last time I have seen him. He nods an apology after Beverly shoots him a dirty look and opens the door.

The winter wind rushes in the house, as cold as when I arrived. Brandon wraps Joy's scarf tighter, and we venture out into the frigid air. Grey clouds have moved in, creating a darker feel than almost noon.

"Looks like snow," I say as my nose begins twitching. I have no idea why, but my nose can almost always tell when snow is coming. My mother swears it is my artistic nature that has me in tune with the weather around me, but I've always wished it would have picked a different way of alerting me. The twitchy nose always makes me want to sneeze.

"Oh, I hope it snows. We never get snow in Dallas." Joy spreads her arms and turns in a circle as if the snow is already falling and she is spinning in it. "I can't wait to see how it feels."

My head drops forward in surprise. "You mean you've never seen snow?"

She shakes her head, her eyes serious under her pink fuzzy hat. "Only on television, but I've always wanted to."

"Well, if it snows, I will come help you build the best snowman after church tomorrow."

"Yay," she shouts the word and accompanies it with a skip around each of us. Her exuberance and joy is contagious. Even Brandon cracks a smile, but then again, he always seems to have one for his daughter.

As we near the diner, Max steps out the door, grunting under his breath, and flips his sign to closed. He has a heavier flannel shirt on today, but no coat and his faded ball cap is in its trademark place turned backward on his head.

"Are you going to the festival, Max?" I don't mean to sound so surprised, but big crowds have never been Max's thing.

He rolls his eyes. "Layla roped me into judging this year, so I have to go. Not that I want to. Got better things to do here." He hooks a finger back toward his diner.

I stifle a laugh at his predicament. "But Max, everyone is going to be at the festival. No one would be coming in anyway."

He shrugs and harrumphs in his usual manner, but joins us in the short walk to the town barn. Joy stares at him with wide eyes as if unsure whether to be afraid of him or amused by him, which brings another smile to my face.

Country music flows from the barn before we hit the front door. An actual old barn, the building is now a faded red. The inside stalls were removed years ago to open up the floor for larger events. Paula uses the space for her dance recitals, but it also serves as the meeting place for town halls and festivals like today.

"There better not be dancing," Max grumbles as he pulls open the door.

The lights inside are bright, illuminating the large structure and the booths set up inside. A heat wave rolls out to meet us, sending a shiver down my spine as it collides with the cold outside.

"Wow," Joy says, and for once her energy is stilled. Her eyes dart back and forth but her feet seem rooted to the spot.

To the left is the popcorn booth. Paula has squeezed her voluptuous frame into a tight red dress, and is eating about as much popcorn as she is popping with the air popper that is plugged into some unseen outlet with a long orange extension cord.

Trudy's table is next, a popup table sporting a myriad of different colored paints, aprons, and wood ornaments. Trudy herself is clad in her overalls – a stark contrast to Paula's formal dress.

A few feet from Trudy, Bert, in his button-down gingham-checked shirt and bow tie, stares down into a crock pot, which I assume holds wax. He dips a string in the pot, squeals in pain, and plunges his finger into his mouth.

A chuckle escapes my lips as I continue scanning the room. There is a table across the back lined with pies and hot chocolate. To the right are tables to sit at, a wreath making table, and Justin playing the music on his computer.

"Where do you want to go first?" Brandon asks Joy, masking his own annoyance though I can see it in his eyes.

Her eyes jump from one place to the next. "There." She points to Trudy, and I am pleased. Artistic outlets are right up my alley.

Trudy raises her eyebrows at me as we approach, and I shake my head a tiny bit in an effort to tell her I'll spill all later.

"Well, who is this angel?" she says, staring at Joy.

"I'm Joy. Who are you?"

I'm surprised by her lack of shyness.

Trudy smiles back. "I'm Trudy. What would you like to paint?"

Joy scans the offerings. Trudy has carved out bells, trees, stars, and plump Santas. Her hand hovers over each as if she can't decide before she picks up the tree. Trudy hands her a brush and pours some green, yellow, and red paint in tiny tubs. Joy dips the brush cautiously in the green and begins to sweep it across her tree.

Unable to help myself, I pick up a Santa and a brush and begin coloring my own. Brandon and Beverly watch in amusement. The flicker of annoyance leaves Brandon's eyes as he watches Joy finish the green and then dot the lights with meticulous strokes.

"She's a natural," Trudy says, and I can't help but agree.

"Can we get a real tree this year, Daddy?" Joy's voice is hopeful as she turns her big eyes up at Brandon. He laughs in response.

"Yes, this year we can get a real tree."

"In fact," I say, "why don't we take her to the farm you took me my first year?"

He cocks his head as if trying to remember; then his eyes light up. "Oh yeah. Okay, tomorrow evening?"

"I'd love to. The shop closes at six, so we can go any time after that."

I catch Joy looking from her father to me and the tiny smile that alights on her lips.

After ornaments, we string some popcorn. I am thankful that Paula keeps her leering eyes off Brandon. It probably helps that he is nearly half her age.

We even stop at Bert's candle making table, though he has forgotten some important element and we are unable to make a candle. The faux pas is typical Bert, but a part of me still feels a little sorry for him.

"Brandon Scott, is that you?" The shrill voice is unmistakable. It is Krissy, the high school cheerleader who dated Brandon on and off throughout high school. Though not her lithe, slender self, the years have been good to her, and she is still as pretty as ever.

"Hi, Krissy, how are you?" Brandon's voice is stiff, almost hesitant as if he is afraid she will try to hit on him.

"I'm good. I married Tony, he worked on the school newspaper, remember? We have one child so far and another on the way." She pats her nearly flat stomach as she says this. It must be very early or else she doesn't show much until later.

"That's wonderful, Krissy," I say, jumping in. "Congratulations."

"Daddy, is it pie time?" Joy asks tugging on Brandon's sleeve.

"Sorry, I guess we have to go, but it was good to see you Krissy."

"Yes, we'll have to get some of the old gang together sometime," she says.

Brandon nods, but it is noncommittal, and I can tell he won't be setting up a meeting anytime soon.

We continue toward the back and Joy's eyes dance in excitement as she nears the pie table. There are a myriad of pies decorating the table – apple, cherry, chocolate, pecan, and pumpkin. She licks her lips as she surveys the offerings. "Can we try them all?"

The laugh that bursts from his lips reminds me of old times. Joyful and full. "No, that would ruin your dinner, but we can each pick a pie and share. How's that?"

Her head nods enthusiastically as she reaches for a large cherry slice.

"Did you enter a pie?" Brandon asks me as he debates over which slice to pick.

I shake my head. "I forgot about the festival until Trudy reminded me, but I don't think it would be fair for me to enter anyway."

"Probably right." Brandon smiles and selects an apple slice. Beverly grabs a pumpkin, and I take a chocolate. Then Brandon fills us each a cup of steaming hot chocolate, and we take our goodies to an empty table.

The Porter family who owns the General Store is sitting at a table near us. They have a large brood with five children, the youngest in diapers. Sid Porter was a few years older than Brandon and me and took over the store after his father retired. His sister, Misty, was a grade younger than us, and she married out of college and only returns for holidays.

Max is sitting at another table along with Barnard, the mayor, and Layla. Max has his usual grumpy stare on as he tastes the pies. Barnard is treating each one like a wine tasting, delicately chewing each bite and tilting his head back and forth before marking on his pad. Layla is simply cleaning up each dessert. I have never seen a woman eat so much and stay as thin as she does, but it might be from the fact that she never seems to slow down.

I take a few bites of my chocolate and then pass it to the right as Joy's pie comes to me. In this manner, we sample a little of each pie without feeling too gluttonous, though my stomach still bulges against my jeans as we finish.

"Let's dance, Daddy." Joy grabs his hand and pulls him over to the makeshift dance floor. As it's really the part Paula uses for her dance recitals, there is a mirror behind them that allows me to see Brandon's face as he twirls around with his daughter.

"You still care for him, don't you?" Beverly's voice breaks my daydream of dancing in Brandon's arms, and a blush crawls across my face.

I open my mouth to answer her, but Joy and Brandon return at that moment. "Presley, may I have this dance?"

Brandon holds out his hand to me and finishes the gesture with a bowing flourish. How different he seems from the man who walked in an hour ago. Small town magic. I place my hand in his and happen to catch the wink Beverly throws my direction.

The music changes to a slow song as we hit the floor, but Brandon doesn't skip a beat. His left hand closes over my right as his arm circles my waist. When he pulls me closer, my body aligns with his, and I can feel every curve of him. His scent – dark and woodsy fills my nose. I want to lean my head on his shoulder, but I don't know if it would be appropriate, so I close my eyes and focus on the feel of his hand on mine and the heat radiating between our bodies.

Though we had danced in high school, this time feels different. Is it the difference in our age? Is it the unspoken of past between us?

When my eyes open, Brandon's deep brown eyes are there, staring down at me. There is an intensity in them I have never seen before. My breath catches, and my lips part following a will of their own. Brandon's grip tightens on my back, and his head begins to lean down.

"Daddy."

The spell is broken as Joy hurries up to us. Brandon pulls back, dropping my hand and running his hand over his bearded chin.

"They're about to award a winner." She grabs his hand and pulls him back to the table where Beverly sits. I follow, trying to erase the almost kiss from my mind.

Barnard stands on the makeshift stage they have brought in and taps the microphone. "Can you hear me?" His voice echoes around the room, and he takes a step back to lessen the volume. Dressed in slacks and a button-down shirt that barely covers his rotund belly, Barnard is that man who sees one thing in the mirror while the rest of us see something different. I've always admired his confidence even if I haven't admired his wardrobe choice.

"Thank you all for coming out today. I hope you enjoyed the festival so far. Everything seems to have been a hit except for Bert's candles."

"I did my best," Bert shouts from the crowd. "I was working with my dead Aunt Frannie's recipe, and I think she forgot to write something down."

A titter of laughter scatters through the crowd.

"Anyway," Barnard draws the words out to grab our attention again. "Feel free to go back and do more crafts. I think we'll have to get more popcorn, but the booths will be open another few hours. Then tonight, you can come back for the Star Lake dance. We're going to clear this floor and kick up our heels." A cheer erupts from the small crowd, and Barnard raises his hands to quiet them.

"Now, the moment you've all been waiting for. I, and my humble associates, have finished tasting all the pies, and we have decided on the winner." He pulls three index cards out of the pocket of his shirt. "In third place, we have Paula's pumpkin pie."

"Ooh, thank you," Paula says pushing her way to the front. Even as she accepts the ribbon, her eyes are scanning the crowd, probably looking for her next victim.

"In second place, we have Bert's cherry pie."

"Aha, at least Aunt Frannie got that recipe right," Bert says, pointing his finger at the ceiling.

Barnard rolls his eyes and shakes his head. I sneak a glance at Brandon, who smiles back at me. Some things never change. Our glance holds a moment longer, and I wonder if he is thinking about that almost kiss as much as I am.

"And first place goes to my apple pie."

"You can't award your own pie, Barnard," Trudy calls from the crowd.

"Well Max and Layla voted as well," he says, puffing up like a turkey. "It's not like I was the sole judge." This is another common occurrence. Barnard has a habit of always entering contests and making sure he wins.

"It's not right," Trudy says, but most of the crowd has lost interest.

"What did I miss?" Anna says, popping in between us.

"Everything," Brandon says. "The festival is basically over."

Beverly glances down at her watch. "Well, I have to go check on your father." After hugging Joy, she waves goodbye to the rest of us and hurries out of the door.

"Can we go to Star Lake?" Joy asks once again bouncing on her feet. The sugar in the pies must have given her a new burst of energy.

Brandon opens his mouth and looks from me back to Joy.

"How about I take her?" Anna asks, sensing something in the air though she missed the near kiss. "I want some time to get to know my niece anyway."

Relief floods Brandon's face, and he mouths "thank you" to Anna, who smiles, looks at me with raised eyebrows, and then grabs Joy's hand.

"Why aren't you coming Daddy?"

Her innocent question flusters him, and a smile forms on my lips as I watch him struggle to come up with an excuse. "Well, um, Presley is going to give me a tour of the town to show me how much has changed."

I cover my mouth to hide the laugh bubbling in my throat. It's a good thing Joy is only five, or she would realize there isn't much to this town and definitely not much that has changed in four short years.

"But I'll be back soon, okay?"

She nods, accepting his lame excuse as gospel and heads out the door with Anna leaving Brandon and I staring at each other.

"So, a tour, huh?" I don't even try to hide the humor in my voice.

"I wanted to have a chance to talk with you and with a five-year-old, that is often hard."

The gaze in his eyes is different, more serious. It sends my heart fluttering and the words running from my mind, so that all I can do is nod and smile.

I wave goodbye to Trudy who catches my eye as we walk toward the door. Her eyebrows raise, and she nods knowingly. Warmth floods my cheeks once again.

Chapter Eight - Brandon

Glancing at Presley as I open the door, I wonder what I'm doing. I don't plan to stay here, but there is no denying the attraction building between Presley and me. Maybe, if she feels the same way, she'll come with us back to Dallas and wherever my job might lead me.

The temperature has dropped while we've been inside, and Presley burrows into her coat. Her hat is pulled low over her ears, hiding her hair. I adjust my own hat, thankful for the beard that covers my face and provides an extra layer of warmth.

Presley's face turns up to the sky, revealing her perfectly smooth white neck. I force myself to refrain from pulling her into my arms right then. Her nose twitches. "The snow is coming," she says.

I used to tease her about this gift, but she was right more often than not, and I learned to take her word. "I don't mind a little snow, do you?"

She shakes her head, a soft smile on her lips. How have I forgotten those perfectly pink lips?

"What happened with Morgan?" she asks, breaking the silence. Her eyes widen as the words tumble out, as if she didn't mean for them to pass her lips.

Sighing, I shove my hands deeper in my pocket, sending my shoulders up near my ears as we continue down Main Street. "I don't really know. I thought we were happy, but she said she wanted more. She wasn't cut out for life in the small town."

Presley's eyes cloud with sympathy. "Is that why you moved?"

"Yeah, after Morgan left, I just couldn't stay, and I think I wanted more too. I wanted to see the world, to make a statement, get back to reality. Dallas seemed like a good first step."

"I'm sorry," she says, though her mouth opens again as if she wants to say more, but nothing comes out.

I shrug, no longer wanting to dwell on my past, but curious as to hers. "It is what it is. What about you? What really happened with the guy in France?"

Her shoulders rise as she takes a deep breath. Her tongue darts out and swipes her bottom lip. I turn my head away as the desire to taste her lips ignites within me.

"He wasn't capable of seeing just me, and I just couldn't make myself stay, so I came home, to the last place I felt really comfortable."

My hand reaches out, as if with a mind of its own, and grasps her arm, halting our forward movement. "Presley, I . . ."

The blue in her eyes brightens, like the clear ocean on a sunny day. "Yes?" Her voice is a whisper, choked back by emotion.

"Will you go to the dance with me tonight?"

She blinks, and I can tell that isn't what she expected to hear. It isn't what I expected to say. I wanted to tell her that I've missed her, that she's beautiful and that just being near her is sending my heart into an overzealous beating.

A snowflake lands on her cheek, and her eyes widen. Another hits her nose, creating a tiny wet dot on the end. As I look up, one lands in my eye, causing me to blink and rub it out.

"I told you it would snow." Her laughter is pure happiness as she throws open her arms and spins in a slow circle. The snow picks up and surrounds her, creating the image of a figurine in a snow globe. She is exotic and hauntingly beautiful against the backdrop of white flakes, and before I know it, my hand has reached out and grabbed hers.

I can't feel her skin through our gloves, but the material doesn't stop the heat generating between us. Her eyes, still dancing with delight, meet mine, and I know there will be no stopping the kiss this time. I pull her the few feet between us, closing the distance. My hand winds around her back, and though no words are said, everything is communicated in our locked gaze.

A tentative smile parts her lips, and that is all the permission I need. Pushing ever so slightly with my body, I lean her back against my arm and place my lips on hers. They are as soft as I expected, and I wonder how my beard feels against her cheek. I hope it isn't too scratchy.

Her arms reach up around my neck as her lips part farther and the kiss deepens. My arm tightens, drawing her closer and for a moment I curse the snow. No, not the snow, just the cold temperature that has us bundled in heavy coats. The snow I love as it falls softly around us. A stillness fills the air and imprints the moment on my mind.

Her eyes are foggy as she opens them again, and I hope I haven't overstepped.

"Well, that was better than I always dreamed it would be," she says.

I stand her back straight, but keep my arm close around her. "What do you mean always?"

Her eyes crinkle with kindness. "Brandon, I've wanted to kiss you since that Christmas we got the tree."

Now it is my turn to blink. I had no idea she had feelings for me back then. "Why didn't you ever tell me?"

Her gloved hand cradles my cheek, and her eyes caress my face. "Because there was always someone else, Brandon."

I open my mouth to protest but realize she is right. What she doesn't know though is that all those other women were my way of trying to mask my feelings for her. I knew within a few months of us becoming friends that I had feelings for her, but I was too afraid of ruining the friendship. Presley had always had a way of getting me to open up and relax that no one else had been able to do.

When I had realized that, an unnatural fear of losing her friendship had covered me, and I had decided not to pursue my feelings for her, but now there was nothing stopping me. We hadn't spoken over the last five years, so there was nothing to lose, and my feelings were just as strong for her, so there was everything to gain.

"I never told you, but I had feelings for you back then too, but was too afraid of losing you. The irony is I ended up losing you anyway. I'm sorry, Presley."

Her finger moves to my lips, stilling them. "It's too late for regrets, but it's not too late for us."

As the snow continues to fall, I pull her in for another kiss, this one slow and lingering. I want to taste everything about her. The heat builds between us, creating a shield between us and the snow, until my phone begins ringing in my pocket.

Frustrated, I break the connection and reach into my pocket. Presley doesn't seem upset. In fact, she is smiling at my annoyance. "Hello?" I say, punching the answer button without looking at the caller ID. I'm expecting my assistant's voice, but the voice of my mother answers me.

"Brandon? They're releasing your father. Can you come help me bring him home? He's still very weak."

Instantly my demeanor changes, and Presley's eyes widen with questions. "Of course, Mom, I'll be right there."

"Is your dad okay?" Presley asks as I end the call.

"Yeah." The word comes out like a sigh though I hadn't realized I was holding my breath. "They're releasing him, but my mother needs help getting him home."

"I'll come with you."

"You don't have to. It won't be very interesting, and I may not make it back in time for the dance."

Her hand squeezes my arm. "Brandon, I want to come with you."

Inside, my heart soars. I don't want to end our day so soon, and the hospital holds no fond memories for me. "Thank you."

Hand in hand, we walk back down Main Street to Cooper Street and then up the road to my parent's house. As we enter the house, the sound of Joy and Anna in the kitchen carries to us. I'm glad she is in out of the cold.

Inside the kitchen, Joy is pressed against the back glass window, and Anna sits at the kitchen table nursing a coffee and coloring. She looks up as we enter and winks.

"Daddy, it's snowing." Joy squeals and turns from the window long enough jump up and down in an excited little dance.

"I know, Pumpkin," I say to her before turning to Anna. "Dad is getting released, so Presley and I are going to help Mom. Can you watch Joy a little longer?"

"Sure." She takes a sip of her coffee, which makes me want to pour a mug of my own. I grab a travel mug from the cabinet and fill it up.

"You want any?" I ask Presley.

"Do you have any creamer?" she asks. "I never got used to drinking it black. I prefer my coffee tan."

Leave it to Presley to have to be unique. It's another thing that has always attracted me to her. Though the chunk in her hair has not always been purple, it has always been a color different from her natural dirty blond. Her nails are typically painted in some sparkly polish, and even her clothes are often brighter than most people would choose to wear, but somehow on her it works. Most people probably saw her as an oddity with her quiet nature yet sparkly exterior, but I knew the real Presley who was somewhere in between the two.

Opening the fridge, I find some white chocolate creamer in the door. She nods her approval as I hold it up, and I rescue another travel mug from the counter and fill it up for her along with a healthy dash of the creamer. The coffee is indeed a light tan color when I hand it to her.

She takes a long sip, closing her eyes in delight as she swallows. The look on her face sends my heart pumping again. Images of morning coffee breaks following blissful nights flood my mind. I force my eyes away from her soft pink lips though all I really want to do is cover them with my own again. A subtle head shake clears my thoughts, and I grab my keys from the hook that hangs on the wall and my coffee, though the heat from my thoughts has chased away the cold.

"Back in a minute, Pumpkin. Be good for Anna."

"Okay," she says, but her face is still pressed to the glass. It doesn't snow in Dallas, but Joy has always been fascinated. I hope it snows enough for her to play in it tomorrow.

Presley follows me out of the kitchen and to my car. Opening her door, I take a moment to steal another kiss. With her back pressed against the car, she grabs my coat with her free hand and pulls me closer. I can almost feel her heart beating through the thick fabric that separates us. Too soon, but for my own sanity, the kiss ends, and we climb into the car.

Her hand finds mine as I start the car, and I shoot her a smiling glance. It is nice having her in the car with me. Even after all the years apart, her presence still soothes and calms me.

"Joy is amazing," she says as we pull onto Main street. The snow is still falling, though lightly, and the street is empty. Everyone must be inside their homes bundled up.

"Yeah, she is."

"Do you want more?" Her voice is tentative and soft.

"More what? Kids?" My eyes flicker from the road to her face for a moment. She nods, but her eyes are cast down on her lap as if she is afraid of my answer. "I honestly haven't thought about it."

Though that is only half true. I have thought about how another child would impact my work and make it that much harder, but that was before Presley re-entered my life. Maybe if the situation were right, I'd be open to another child.

We arrive at the hospital a few minutes later. My father's face is still shocking, and I squeeze Presley's hand as I hear her soft gasp beside me. His left eye is now a faded purple, but still swollen. There are stitches across the back of his head where they'd had to drill a hole to relieve the initial pressure, and he is thinner. He looks as if he has lost twenty pounds as his shirt hangs loosely on him, and his pants require a belt to stay up.

My mother's eyebrow raises at Presley's and my clasped hands, and a smile pulls across her lips.

"Mr. Scott, I'm so happy to hear you are coming home," Presley says.

My father turns his good eye to her. "Is that Presley Hays? Thank you for the treats."

"You are welcome, sir."

The orderly arrives a moment later and helps load my father into a wheelchair. He, of course, protests the whole time, declaring his ability to walk even as his legs shake against the foot petals.

We stay with him while my mother gets her car. As she pulls up in front of the hospital door, my father attempts to stand and collapses back in the chair. I take one arm and Presley takes the other. His face furrows as if he is about to protest, but then his lips flatten into a line, and he shuffles forward.

It is a slow walk the ten or fifteen feet out of the hospital to where Mother has parked the car, but my father is out of breath when we arrive. My eyes are full of concern as I glance at my mother. Though I knew my father had taken a nasty fall, I am not used to seeing him so weak and helpless.

She nods once to let me know she is aware but smiles, assuring me that everything will be alright.

Presley can sense my unease as we drive home. Her hand lands on my arm. "Don't worry. He'll be okay. Sometimes it just takes a little longer to heal. I'll be praying for his speedy recovery."

I know she is trying to help, but at this moment, I just want to not think about my father. "After we help get him inside, how about we go to that dance after all? I could use a distraction."

Nodding, she squeezes my knee, and that simple gesture sends a flood of peace through my body. I've missed having Presley in my life.

Chapter Nine - Presley

I glance in the mirror at the blue dress I have chosen. It is knee length, and has a line of flowers around the neckline. Simple, but dressy. I grab a cardigan in case it gets chilly in the barn and throw my coat over my arm so that I will be ready when Brandon arrives.

The knock sounds precisely at seven pm. Brandon has not lost his need to be punctual. A smile is already on my face as I open the door, but it lengthens at the sight of him. Though I cannot tell what he is wearing underneath his heavy coat and hat, I can see his eyes and the smile behind his beard.

"You look beautiful," he says, taking my hand and stepping into the apartment.

As he pulls me close, I can smell his cologne — a mixture of sandalwood and a clean scent like the ocean. My hand pushes his hat back so I can run my fingers through his hair and then caresses his cheek. I wasn't sure I would like his beard, but it is softer than it looks. When my fingers touch his lips, he grabs them and moves them over his heart before placing his lips against mine. Heat flames through my body as the kiss deepens.

"We better get to the dance or we may never make it out of here," he says, his voice breathless and husky.

Recovering from the emotions flooding my body, I can only nod and slip into my coat. Being around Brandon is intoxicating, and I will have to be vigilant not to let it go too far.

The snow has stopped for now, but a layer of white lays about the town. I love the snow like this, when the air is crisp and cold and everything looks pure and new. It isn't quite enough snow to build a snowman with Joy as I promised, but I'm hopeful it will snow some more. If my itchy nose is any indication, it will.

Brandon's fingers lace through mine as we begin the walk to the barn. The town is quiet. It looks different in the dark with few places lit up. Even Max's diner is dark as we near it. I have a hunch that Layla has dragged him to the dance, though he will probably pretend to be annoyed by it.

There are strings of white Christmas lights hanging from the trees near the barn and several strands hung back and forth across the front of the building. Either someone has hung them since the festival or else I hadn't noticed them earlier.

Music carries on the still air — a lively teeny bopper tune that makes me wonder if they have raided Justin's CD collection from a few years ago.

"Oh, dear, are we sure we want to do this?" Brandon asks, but the smile on his face belays his amusement and softens his words.

The inside of the barn has been transformed again. The tables and the CD player are still on one side, but the other side has been cleared of the pop up tables, allowing for more dance floor space.

Trudy waves from across the room and then raises her camera and snaps a shot.

I return the wave as Brandon pulls me toward an empty table where we shed our coats. At the back wall, a row of potluck food lines a long table. As my eyes take in the savory casseroles and bowls of salads, my stomach rumbles, and I realize I haven't eaten in a few hours.

"Can we get some food?"

"Already ahead of you," he says laughing. "Why do you think I chose the table right by the food?" They say the fastest way to a man's heart is through his stomach, and whether that is true or not, Brandon has always enjoyed food.

As we join the dozen other people in the line for the food, I sneak a look at Brandon. His green button-down shirt hugs his broad shoulders and tapers down to a narrow waist. It is tucked into a pair of black slacks that skim the curves of his lower body, hinting at what lies beneath.

After grabbing some salad and a casserole chunk which resembles lasagna, we return to the table to see that Bert and Amelia, the quiet girl who runs the flower shop have joined us. In traditional Bert flair, he is sporting a brown bow tie over a green checkered shirt. His hair is parted on the side and flattened down, but like Alfalfa, he has one finicky cowlick that stands on end at the back of his head.

Amelia's eyes are focused on her plate as she shifts a piece of salad back and forth across the plate. Her shyness is an odd contrast to Bert's outgoing persona. Her brown hair is curled into ringlets and pulled back with a white flowered headband.

"Presley, you might know. What would you think about me offering a taxi service for animals like Lyft?" Bert asks as he shoves a giant piece of bread in his mouth.

"I don't know much about Lyft, but where would animals need to go?" I ask, pursing my lips to keep from smiling.

"I would take dogs from their homes to daycare and back."

"Who would you drive? There is no dog daycare around here." Brandon rolls his eyes as he sits down.

Bert's head turns as he ponders this. "I could drive them out of town I suppose, but my sister's car is not very reliable."

Brandon and I share an amused glance and continue eating our food. If nothing else, Bert's ideas are always good for a laugh.

When our plates are empty, Brandon grabs my hand and pulls me to the dance floor. As his arms circle mine, my heart accelerates. I can feel the muscles in his arm through his thin shirt, and the chiseled features of his chest when he tightens his grip, pulling me closer. His eyes are staring into mine, daring me to get lost in the chocolate pools that reside there.

My throat closes, and it is hard to swallow. I could live here, safe in Brandon's arms. The feeling is natural, organic until his ringing phone interrupts it.

"Sorry, I have to take this."

And just like that, the mood is broken. His face hardens back into the stiff posture I saw the first day, and without a second glance, he leaves me on the dance floor and heads to the entrance of the barn. His phone is already attached to his ear as he winds through the dancing couples.

Trudy arrives at my side moments later. "What happened?"

I shrug, tears pricking my eyes. "Work, I think, but he didn't really say." I hope it is just work, but my mind is thinking back to the last conversation I had with Pierre.

I sit on the small terrace, sipping a cup of tea and staring at the Eiffel Tower lit up in the distance. Tonight is my last night in Paris. It has been an amazing few years studying baking and then working in the city of lights, and I am going to miss it.

"I do not want you to go," Pierre says, joining me at the little table and handing me a small cup of my favorite dessert, chocolate mousse. Breathing in the heavenly scent, I flash him a warm smile. We met a year ago at a bistro. He had been reading the paper and watching me as I devoured my first chocolate mousse. After my second, he had come over to her table, explaining he had to meet the woman who so enjoyed her dessert. Though mortified, I allowed him to join me at the table, and it became the first of many dates. While I knew we would never marry, he had filled the hole in my heart that

had existed since leaving Brandon, at least until I had seen him with another woman.

"I know," I say, "but my time here is up." Scooping a delicate spoonful of the fluffy brown dessert, I close my eyes as the spoon enters my mouth. I have never figured out why, but the chocolate mousse here lights up my taste buds and sets my pulse racing. One day, I hope to be able to duplicate it in my own shop.

"What will I do without ma Cheri?" Pierre stands and crosses behind me, his hands landing on my shoulders, gently massaging them.

A shiver travels down my spine. There are some things about Pierre I will miss, and the feel of his lips on my neck is one of them. "I'm sure you'll go back to all your other women," I say, trying to remain in control. Though I say the words lightly, they sting even as they leave my mouth. It is only a suspicion, but I think he is cheating on me. Perhaps if he thinks I know, he will admit it to me.

"But they will not be you," he whispers in my ear.

And there it is. The reason I can never stay with him. I had seen him with a buxom blond two weeks ago, but they hadn't appeared overly friendly. However, the next day my friend, Minuet, informed me that she saw him stealing kisses with a blond. Her description closely matched the woman I had seen him with, though I hadn't told her about the sighting. I knew then it was time to leave, and put my notice in and began packing up.

"I have to go see my family again," I say softly, changing the subject. There's no reason to fight about the other woman. Pierre never said we were exclusive and somehow here in France, a woman or two on the side is more acceptable, though it is not acceptable to me. "It's been years, and I miss them." Another spoonful of mousse finds its way to my mouth, and I sigh. Though Pierre is no longer one of them, there are things I will miss about France.

"I could come with you," Pierre says, his breath tickling my ear.

The words snap my eyes open. I do not want Pierre coming with me. "You would hate it, Pierre," I say trying to keep my voice even. "The food isn't nearly as good, and I'll have to be living with my mom

and younger brother for a while until I can get my own place again."
Ryan works in Houston, Pierre doesn't need to know that.

His hands leave my shoulders and he circles the table, sitting in the other seat. Placing his chin on folded hands, he stares into my eyes. Those eyes – they are my weakness and he knows it. With his dark hair, he reminds me very much of Brandon, which is probably why I fell for him in the first place, but his eyes are an arresting blue, the color of the ocean after a storm, and they are what has kept me coming back. I will miss those eyes.

"I think you are trying to convince me not to come," he says in his lilting accent, "but I agree. I do not think I would like what you are describing. So, I suppose tonight is goodbye."

Though he stays a little longer, he seems anxious to leave now that our dating relationship is over. When he does finally bid good night, I feel a flood of relief. After another longing look at the city that has been my home for the last few years, I step back inside the flat to finish packing. It is going to be a long flight home.

"I don't think I will be able to take it if there's another woman on the side."

My hands are shaking as Trudy leads me back over to the table. Thankfully Bert and Amelia are dancing, and we are alone.

"Oh, girl, that cheating Pierre affected you more than you're letting on, didn't he?"

I nodded; I had told Trudy just a little about what happened with Pierre.

"Well, I don't think Brandon is like that." Trudy's voice is soft as she places a hand on my arm. "Did he ever date multiple women in high school?"

I shake my head no. I'm really not even worried that it's another woman. In fact, I'm a little more worried that it's not, because if it is his job, it will be even harder to compete with. "Work can be a mistress too."

My voice is soft, but she hears the words, and her eyes widen in understanding. Then her eyebrow raises, and she nods behind me. I know without even looking that Brandon has returned.

"Sorry about that," he says sliding in the chair next to me. "It was my assistant, but I think everything is worked out. She shouldn't bother us any more tonight."

He is trying to make me feel better. I can tell from his tone, and while I'm still worried about my fragile heart, I decide to try and enjoy the rest of the evening. "Okay, shall we finish dancing then?"

"I thought you'd never ask."

He takes my hand once again, and I shoot a final glance at Trudy, who smiles and nods. If she believes that it won't overpower our relationship, then I guess I can too.

As Brandon pulls me close on the dance floor, the fear begins to abate, and I find myself once again wrapped up in his safe arms. I lean my head against his shoulder, enjoying the solidity of it and the slight tickling of his beard on my forehead.

His phone does not ring the rest of the night, and I allow myself to believe it was a one-time thing. When the dance ends, we gather our coats and head out into the cold night with the rest of the crowd.

"Oh, come on, Max, you know you had fun," I hear Layla say off to my right.

"Or how about a cat day care? You know like a dog one, only for cats?" Bert's voice carries from the left.

Giggling, I snuggle into the crook of Brandon's arm, and he pulls me closer. "I bet you don't see that in Dallas," I say pointing to the sky above, clear and filled with stars.

"That you don't," he says, "but we have other things that you can't get here."

I kick myself as I hear his voice shift. I don't want him thinking about what he's missing. It is clear I still have my work cut out for me.

Chapter Ten - Presley

After church the next day, I stop by Max's and grab sandwiches to take to Brandon's house. I don't know if they've gone to a different church or even if they've had lunch, but I feel the need to show up with something.

Max eyes me as he puts the wrapped sandwiches in a paper bag. There is something on his mind evident from his frownier than usual face and slightly pursed lips.

"What?" I ask with a sigh when he doesn't offer his thoughts.

"I just wonder if you know what you're getting yourself into. I don't want you sitting in my corner table scaring the customers away again when he leaves."

It had only been two days, right after Brandon told me about Morgan, that I had sat in his corner table, eating ice cream and sketching, refusing to talk to anyone, but Max had let me know in no uncertain terms that I had affected his bottom line and should take my sulking elsewhere.

"I'm not getting into anything," I say, trying to convince myself as much as Max. "It's just lunch with his family."

His eyebrow raises, but he says nothing more as he finishes filling the paper bag and pushes it across the counter to me. Plopping down two twenties, I pick up my bag.

"What about your change?" he asks as I head toward the door.

"Put it on my tab for next time," I call, pushing the door open to the white wonderland outside. The snow is still falling lightly outside as I head to Cooper Street.

Though not heavy, the bag is awkward, and I end up shifting it several times from one hip to the other before reaching Brandon's house. He opens the door before my finger can hit the bell, and my eyes widen in surprise.

"I listened for the step," he reveals, his grin reaching across his face. He takes the bag from me, and I stomp the snow off my boots before crossing the threshold into the house. After carefully removing my hat, coat, and scarf, I hang them on the rack and follow him into the kitchen.

"Presley brought lunch," Brandon says as we enter.

"Oh, good, I'm starving," Anna exclaims, shutting the book she had been reading and jumping up to open the pantry in search of paper plates.

"I want to build a snowman," Joy says.

"Let's eat," I tell her, "and I'll help you build a good one after lunch."

"You promise?" The question catches me off guard, but it's the look in her eyes that really bothers me, as if she is often used to having promises broken. I sneak a glance at Brandon, but he isn't paying attention. He is busy emptying the bag and doling out the sandwiches.

"I promise." I drop down to my knees to be on eye level with Joy. "Building snowmen is one of my favorite pastimes."

Her eyes sparkle. "Mine too, or at least I think it will be after I build my first one."

Laughing, I grab her hand and lead her to the table where Brandon and Anna have laid out plates and sandwiches. Beverly arrives with two bags of chips and cups. Bruce, probably needing to feel useful, pours iced tea in each cup and passes it to his right.

After lunch, I help Beverly clear the table as Brandon takes Joy to add on layers. The snow is still falling, which means the air is still cold outside.

Joy returns a few moments later, walking stiffly with her arms out and her legs straight. A scowl lines her face. "I can't move like this, Daddy."

"But you'll be warm," he says, "which is more important." He is also bundled up, but only in a coat and hat.

"How many layers is she wearing?" I ask, counting at least two from the different colored necklines protruding from her coat.

"Four. She doesn't have a heavy coat, and I don't want her to freeze."

I bite my lips together, stifling a laugh not wanting Joy to think I am laughing at her, but the situation is comical. "Maybe it will loosen up as you move," Hurrying into the living room, as a giggle escapes my lips, I grab my coat, hat, scarf, and boots and hurry back to them.

Brandon holds the coat for me as I shrug my arms into the sleeves, and then he wraps his arms around me, sneaking a quick peck on the cheek before letting go of me. Cheeks still aflame, I pull my hat on and wrap the scarf around my neck. My gloves, tucked safely in my coat pockets, are the last item I add, and then we venture into the backyard.

The snow, while light, has been falling almost steadily since it started last night creating a coating of a few inches on the ground, enough to build a snowman if it's the right kind of snow.

Joy squeals with delight and runs around in circles, stopping every few minutes to stick out her tongue and catch snowflakes. "It's so cold," she says.

While Brandon is watching Joy, I bend down and roll up a ball of snow, pelting him with it before he has time to turn around.

"Hey." His shout is more from surprise than annoyance, but the evil glint appears in his eye. Squealing, I run as he bends down to scoop up his own snowball.

His ammo hits the side of my leg, spraying me with cold pellets. Joy stops to watch us, and after realizing we are playing begins scooping up her own balls and pelting Brandon.

I land another one as he is turned to deal with Joy.

"Hey, no fair," he shouts. "This is two against one."

"That's right," I shout back and dodge his next ball.

Joy lands one on his hip and doubles over with laughter as he pretends to be angry and come after her. She doesn't even try to get away, but allows him to pick her up and swing her around.

"I'll get you later," he says. "Right now, we need to get Presley."

She agrees, and I sprint toward the safety of some bushes, but not fast enough. Brandon's longer stride catches me, and as he grabs for my coat, I lose my footing and fall to the soft snow. Brandon, tripping over my flailing feet, lands on top of me, his face inches from mine. His arms, thankfully, caught his fall or else we might have smashed faces.

I can feel his breath on my face as his eyes stare into mine and begin to close, his face lowering.

"What are you doing?" Joy asks.

Brandon's eyes snap back open, and he scrambles up. "Nothing, Presley and I both fell is all." He holds out his hand to me and helps me up.

"Uh huh, sure," she says eying us both. She is smart and can tell something is different, but she appears unsure what to do with her information. "Can we build the snowman now?"

"Yes," I say, trying to calm my racing heart. "Let's do this." Bending down, I begin to push the snow into a ball shape. It is not quite as wet as it should be and pieces of snow keep falling off the ball, creating more of a lopsided circle.

Brandon begins pushing with me as the ball gets bigger, his eyes stealing furtive glances. When the base is made, we pause to catch our breath, and Joy brings snow over to patch the holes. There is a large winding trail of green grass behind us contrasting with the white snow-covered rest of the backyard.

After the second ball is finished, I notice Joy's teeth chattering. "Let's finish the head quickly," I say softly to Brandon. When he raises his brow at me, I nod my head in Joy's direction. She is stalwartly still bringing snow over, but her nose is bright pink, and she can't keep her teeth locked together.

Brandon deftly rolls up the last smaller ball and places it on the top before turning to Joy. "Okay, little one, let's get you inside and warmed up."

"I'm o. . .o. . .okay," she insists, through teeth still snapping repeatedly together.

"No, you're not. You're freezing. We'll finish dressing the snowman later after you've warmed up."

Though she looks like she wants to protest, the cold wins and Joy nods. Together, we troop back into the house and peel off our cold, wet layers.

Beverly, Anna, and Bruce are nowhere to be seen, so Brandon starts a tea kettle warming on the stove for hot chocolate, and I take Joy into the living room and flick on the electric fireplace.

As she sits, teeth still chattering, I bring her a blanket and wrap it around both of our shoulders. "Is that better?" I ask her. She nods and curls into me. Unsure what to do, I open my arm and allow her to snuggle in.

Moments later, the tea kettle whistles, and Brandon enters bearing a tray with three steaming mugs of hot chocolate. He smiles at our pose before handing the smallest cup to Joy. "Be careful, it's hot."

"I know Daddy." Her nose is returning to its normal color, and she has warmed up enough that she can control her mouth. She pushes away from me and cups the mug with both hands, holding it just under her chin and letting the steam float up to her eyes.

He hands a mug to me, holding my fingers longer than he needs to. I flash a warm smile up at him as he sits beside me. We are silent, sipping our hot chocolate and enjoying the warmth, but it is easy to envision this as a regular occurrence for us. It feels like home for the first time in years.

When the hot chocolate is gone, and we are sufficiently warmed, Joy grabs my hand. "Do you want to put a puzzle together with me?"

Smiling, I follow her over to a card table they have set up for her and am surprised to see a five-hundred-piece puzzle spread out over the table.

"She loves puzzles," Brandon says, coming behind me and placing his hands on my shoulders. It is an innocent gesture, but it sends a chill down my spine. It has been too long since anyone has placed their hands on my shoulders in a show of possession, and it makes me smile. With my left hand, I reach up and squeeze Brandon's hands, while my right searches for a puzzle piece to place.

An hour later the puzzle is finished, and we go off in search of the rest of the family. They have been mysteriously absent for the past few hours.

We find them in the family room, passed out in front of the television, which is playing the highlights of some football game. Putting my finger to my lips, I motion them to follow me out of the room.

"Joy, are you warmed up enough?"

She nods. "I'm toasty."

"How about we go get a tree?"

Her mouth opens, and I fling my finger back to my lips, sure she is about to squeal. She claps a hand over her mouth and nods, eyes wide and dancing.

"Fine, but you need another layer," Brandon says, steering Joy down the hall to the bedrooms.

Her sigh is audible down the hallway, and smiling I head back for my own coat and hat. They are still a little wet from the romp earlier, but I figure I'll be okay. We meet back at the front door and head into the cold.

The snow has stopped, which means the air is slightly warmer, but only slighter. Brandon steers us to his father's pickup parked on the side; his city car would never be able to hold a tree.

After turning the truck on to let Joy and I keep warm, he heads into the shop and returns with a saw and some rope.

Brandon backs out of the drive slowly, partly because of the snow on the ground and partly because Joy isn't in her usual car seat. The forest isn't very far, and there is very little traffic, but Brandon still drives cautiously. His shoulders are hunched forward, and his hands gripping the wheel are white around the knuckles. I can't decide if he is more worried about the snow or the lack of a car seat.

Ten minutes later, he pulls the truck to a stop outside the forest. It is as I remember it. Tall Virginia Pines fill the forest, like an army of green triangles ready to march into battle. They are accompanied by smaller scraggly trees and brush.

We pile out of the truck, and before the doors are shut, Joy takes off running. "Daddy, look at all the trees."

"Find us a good one," he hollers back.

"She sure seems excited," I say, meeting him at the back of the truck.

"Yeah, well there aren't many places to get a real tree in Dallas." The saw swings from his hand as we make our way to the forest.

I try again to picture him in a big city, but can't do it. He fits so well here in this small town where you don't have to try and impress anyone.

"Over here, Daddy. This one."

Joy's voice leads us into the forest, where she stands pointing at a tall tree. It must be nearly eight feet judging by how much taller it is than Brandon who stands at just over six feet.

"Will it fit?" I can't remember how tall the ceilings in his living room are, though I think they are taller than eight feet.

"Yeah, but just barely." He is walking slowly around the tree, perusing every branch and detail. I have forgotten what a tree connoisseur he is. The first year he brought me, he walked around for nearly half an hour before deciding on the perfect tree. "You sure this is the one?"

"Yes, this one." Joy jumps up and down, accentuating her words.

Smiling, Brandon crouches down and begins to saw the thick trunk. The crunching noise of the saw ripping through the bark breaks the stillness and Joy scurries to my side. My arm instinctively surrounds her and pulls her close.

"Here it comes."

The tree begins to tilt our direction, and I move Joy to the side a minute before the tree tumbles down. Brandon saws the ragged edge at the bottom and then he grabs the trunk and begins pulling the tree back toward the truck.

Remembering the last time and the slew of needles we lost, I pick up the end and Joy, pretending to help, places her little hands on the middle and walks with us. At the truck, I place my end in first and then Brandon shoves his end until the tree is securely in the bed. Then he ties the tree down with the rope while Joy and I warm up in the cab.

We repeat the procedure in reverse back at the house, and Anna, hearing the commotion, opens the front door for us.

"I'll go get the tree stand," she says and rushes off, a wide smile on her face.

"I'll get the ornaments," Beverly announces and hurries off toward the attic.

"I'll just sit here, I guess," Bruce grumbles, the agitation at his inability to help clear in his voice.

"You can help us make sure we don't have any holes once we're done decorating." I walk over to him, hoping to offer some words of encouragement. "I know it's hard right now, but at least you're home for Christmas."

Taking my hand, he squeezes it, and smiles.

Chapter Eleven - Brandon

Watching Presley with my father, I can't help but picture the kind of wife and mother she would be. She always seems to know exactly what people need to hear and when they need to hear it.

A tug on my pant leg breaks my daydreaming, and I bend down to Joy, who has motioned me with her little finger. "I like her too Daddy. She's nice."

"Yes, she is, Pumpkin. Yes, she is."

"Are you going to marry her?"

I glance up at Presley, but Joy's voice is soft, and Presley hasn't heard. "I don't know, Joy, but I'd like to see her more. Would that be okay with you?"

She nods, and her eyes light up. "I know what to ask Santa for."

Before I can say anything, she darts out of the room.

"What was that about?" Anna asks, presenting the tree stand to me like a gift.

"I have no idea." I unscrew the tongs that hold the tree in place, and then Anna and Presley join me in lifting the tree and guiding it into the hole. While they hold it steady, I crawl under the tree and screw the tongs back in to hold the tree in place. "Can you get me some water while I'm down here?"

Anna's feet move toward the kitchen and return moments later. She hands down a plastic pitcher filled with water, and I slowly pour it into the base.

Mother returns with the lights and ornaments as I wiggle out from under the tree. She sets the boxes on the couch and then grabs the remote to turn on music. After a few clicks, cheerful Christmas music fills the air.

Presley and I begin untangling the lights and winding them around the tree. Joy returns a moment later, looking like the Cheshire cat with her silly grin, and watches us.

After a few tries, we get the lights on correctly and plugged in. Blue, green, white, and red colors burst forth from their plastic prisons.

"Oooh pretty," Joy says.

With the lights on, we move to the ornaments, taking turns picking one from the box and hanging it on the tree. My father shouts out directions from his chair. "No, a little higher. We need one to the right. There's a hole right by your hand."

It takes a good hour, but finally the tree meets his approval and all of ours. We step back and admire the light as it reflects off the ornaments and reaches into the corners of the room. Presley nudges me with her elbow, a familiar gesture from high school, and I wrap my arm around her and pull her close.

As the smell of her strawberry scented shampoo hits my nose, desire courses through my body. It is hard being this close to her and not being able to shower her with kisses. Her hand splays across my chest, and it takes all my strength not to tug her from the room for a private moment.

The grandfather clock on the wall bongs seven o'clock and Presley jumps. "Oh, dear, I didn't realize it was getting so late. I need to go feed Niko."

My own stomach rumbles at the mention of food, but it can wait until I walk Presley home.

"I'm hungry too, Daddy."

"Why don't you come with me, Joy," my mother says, "and we'll figure out what we can rustle up for dinner."

After Presley bids goodnight to everyone and dons her coat once again, we step out into the chilly night air. My hand finds hers, our fingers intertwining. I can't remember the last time I enjoyed holding hands, but I relish the moment now.

"Are you happy here?" I ask. The air is still and quiet around us; our footsteps crunching in the snow is the only sound.

"Yeah, I think so. It's nice to be home anyway."

Her words pierce my good mood. I was hoping she'd say she missed the city life and wanted to return.

"You seem happy here too," she says, squeezing my hand.

"I'm happy with you." I want to believe it's just her and not this town working its magic on me again. I bought into that fairy tale once and it didn't work out well, but I can't deny there is a pull in this town. There is a simplicity and a friendliness that you don't get in big cities, and a part of me not only misses that but wants something similar for Joy growing up.

Before I have sorted out my thoughts, we reach Presley's apartment. As she turns to face me, I want to throw open her door and carry her into the bedroom, but Presley has always been adamant that she would wait for marriage. I lean into her, pushing her against the door, and take her face in my hands.

My eyes fixate on hers, an ocean of blue. My thumb trails down her cheek and across her lips, which part at my touch. Her chest rises in anticipation, and I wrap my hand around the back of her neck, pulling it to me.

The kiss is urgent in need. I've been teased with the sight and smell of her all day and unable to do anything to satisfy the desire, and the floodgates of passion open. My hand moves from her cheek to the small of her back, pressing her deeper into me. Her body contours against mine, and my heart begins to pound in my head.

Her hands run up my chest, but instead of wrapping around my shoulders or my neck as I hoped, she pushes against my chest, breaking the kiss.

"We need a break," she says, her voice throaty and breathless.

"Presley." Her name is almost a moan on my lips as I lean in again, but she is resolute.

"Brandon, we need a break. I . . . I want to do this right."

Those are not the words I wanted to hear, but I respect Presley, and back off. "You're right," I say, though my body is screaming otherwise. "Thank you for a wonderful day. Can Joy and I come see you tomorrow?"

"I'd like that," she says and places a soft, quick peck on my lips before turning and opening her door. She stands in the doorway, an angel with a purple streak and waves goodbye.

As the door closes and I begin the walk back home, my mind rehashes the day. My life feels so different with Presley in it, but I wonder if I'm falling too fast, and I worry about Joy. What if Presley won't come back with me? I might get over it, but I'm not sure Joy would.

Chapter Twelve - Presley

I am just finishing up arranging the pastries in the display case when the overhead bell jingles.

"Hi, Presley, can I help you today and learn how to bake?" Joy's excited voice carries across the room before I even look up.

"Well, hello Miss Joy."

"I'm sorry, but she really wanted to come see you today, and I need to help Mom around the house a bit. Is it okay if she stays for an hour or so? I'll come back before lunch, I promise." Brandon's face is apologetic and sincere.

"Of course, it's okay," I say. "Come here Joy, and we'll make some cookies."

"Yay, cookies."

As Joy runs behind the display case to see the back, Brandon reaches for my hand. "Thank you for this." He brings my hand to his mouth and brushes the back of it with his lips.

"No problem. Joy is great, and I'm sure we'll be fine."

He holds my eyes a moment longer before reminding Joy to be good and walking out of the shop.

I turn to the brunette angel beside me. "I started baking when I was about your age, so I guess it's time you learn. Okay, we need flour and sugar. Let's go to the back and get some from the pantry."

Her brown eyes, so like Brandon's, widen. "You have a pantry back there?"

"Of course," I chuckle. "Where else would I keep all the ingredients? I also have a big refrigerator and freezer for the cold ingredients."

She grabs my hand as we walk to the large pantry. Her hand is tiny in mine, but her grip is strong. It is obvious she is missing a mother figure. I had guessed it from the amount of time she spent with me yesterday when I swung by after church, but every gesture of hers is confirming it.

"Wow, there's so much stuff in here." Joy's voice brings me back into the present, and I look around the pantry. It is rather large, the size of a large closet, with five shelves reaching from about knee height up to just beyond my head. Sugar, flour, baking soda, baking powder, salt, yeast, and many other dry ingredients line the shelves.

I drop her hand long enough to grab flour, sugar, salt, brown sugar, and vanilla. I hand her the vanilla and the salt, and we head to the mixing table and place our ingredients down. Then it's back to the refrigerator for butter, eggs, and chocolate chips.

The refrigerator, also grand, earns another wide-eyed stare from Joy. I hand her the chocolate chips, and we journey back to the table. As we place the ingredients down, the bell jingles. "Be right back," I say to the little helper and step into the main room.

Layla is there with her daily order of muffins and bread for the inn. I love when she comes in as she keeps me in business. Today she looks super smart in khaki pants and a pink flowered top. Her brown hair skims her shoulders.

"Presley, was that Brandon Scott I saw you with at the dance Saturday night?" Her voice holds just a note of teasing laced with her interest.

"It was. He's back in town for a time to help out his father." I hope she won't say something unfortunate with Joy around.

"Oh, yes, I heard about that. Well, you two looked good together, but then again, I've thought that since you two were in high school. Why did you never date?" Layla was managing the inn when we were in high school, but now she owns it. Though not typically a gossip, she has a pulse on everything that happens in the town.

I shrug in answer to her question. "Timing was never right, I guess." She hands me her list, and I begin boxing up her muffins. Four chocolate, four blueberry, four flax, and one apple cinnamon which I'm almost certain is for her.

"Ah, yes, timing. Well, as you know it took ten years for Max and me to come around. I hope your time is shorter."

"Me too." I chuckle a little because even back in high school, the romance between Layla and Max had been the talk of the town. We all knew Max had liked her – he kept a special seat reserved for her in the diner, yet she had seemed unaware. And there had been rumors she had feelings for him, but she had never told him. I'd have to ask Trudy what finally brought them together as it had happened while I was in Paris.

I finish boxing the muffins and grab the loaves of bread she has requested as well. Two sourdough loaves and one cheddar bread – the bread changes day to day but there is always at least one sourdough. She slides her card across the counter to me, and I hand her the merchandise. After signing her name, she waves, and the bell signals her exit.

"Joy, are you still okay back there?" I'm a little worried as it has been quiet, and though I don't have kids, I grew up with a younger brother, and I know quiet usually means disaster.

"Mmmhmm." Her reply is garbled as if she has a mouth full of something. The chocolate chips. Slapping my head, I hurry back there to find half the bag gone and her cheeks puffed out like a chipmunk.

"Oh, Joy. You are going to get a tummy ache from all that sugar, and your dad is going to have my hide."

Her big eyes turn sad and begin to fill with tears. I hadn't meant it seriously or at least not all seriously, but I have forgotten how literal young children are.

"Joy, don't cry. It's okay. Just spit it out, and I'm sure your tummy will be fine." I'm hoping that is the truth, but I have no idea how much she shoved in her mouth before I caught her. The bag hadn't been full, but I could have sworn it had been three quarters full.

I steer her to the big silver basin sink, and she leans over and opens her mouth. Chocolate chips cascade like barrels over a waterfall out of her mouth. As they keep falling, I wonder how she stuffed that many in her mouth. I'll have to keep a closer eye on her.

"There, that's better," I say, when she is finally done.

"Please don't tell Daddy." Her voice is soft and pleading and pulls on my heartstrings.

"I don't think he would be too mad, honey." My hand pats her hair rhythmically. It is soft, like spun gold, but the color of chocolate. She buries her face in my hip.

"But it will stress him out, and he's working so hard." Her voice hitches; tears won't be far behind.

My heart goes out to her, and I wonder if Brandon has any idea the stress his need to succeed is having on his daughter. My guess is that he doesn't because I can't see him as the type of person who wouldn't care about that. "Okay, Joy, I won't tell him." I won't tell him what happened, but I will be talking to him about the need to spend time with his daughter.

I have firsthand knowledge of this as my father left when I was four. He up and decided he no longer wanted to be a father. My mother, who had been staying home with us, then had to find a job and since my father disappeared off the face of the Earth, she'd had to find two jobs. Though I loved her, I had rarely seen her, and it had caused me to withdraw into my art. It was only meeting Brandon that had finally pulled me out of my shell.

My younger brother had taken the opposite road; he had begun acting out as I tried to be a sister and a mother to him, so I had seen both sides of what can happen when kids don't get enough attention, and I didn't want to see either of these happen to Joy.

"Do we still have enough to make cookies?" She wipes her eyes with her small hand and turns big doe eyes up at me.

"I think we do. I'll grab some peanut butter chips, and we'll add those to make sure. Chocolate and peanut butter make a great combination."

"Thank you, Presley," she says, letting go of my pant leg. "I promise not to eat any more."

"Well, at least not until we're done cooking," I say and ruffle her hair slightly.

After grabbing the peanut butter chips, we begin mixing the ingredients and rolling out the dough. Joy has reverted back to her sunny self, but I am still worried about her and why she shoved the chips in her mouth in the first place.

Chapter Thirteen - Brandon

"Brandon Scott, what do you think you are doing?"

My mother's hands are akimbo on her hips as I step into the living room. I remove my coat and hat and hang them on the rack before turning back to her.

"I'm here to help you with Dad, Mom. What do you mean?" I thought we had covered this last night after I returned from walking Presley home. Is my mother going senile? Will I have to deal with that as well?

"That is not what I am talking about Brandon. I'm talking about Presley."

My brow furrows together. "Presley? What about Presley?" I feel like I've just entered an episode of the Twilight Zone and that my mother started this conversation with another me — a doppelganger or something.

"I'm talking about you leading that poor girl on. Unless you've changed your mind about staying." Her hazel eyes stare at me pointedly, and I am reminded of the feeling when I was five and caught with my hand in the cookie jar.

"You know I haven't, Mother. I'm still working on this promotion, but I'm not leading her on. I'm," I pause as the words that were about to come out of my mouth, I haven't vocalized to anyone.

"If you break her heart again, Brandon, I may beat you myself."

"Again?" Her words halt the direction my mind was going and cause it to turn full circle. "When did I break her heart the first time? We never dated."

She stares at me, her anger softening to disbelief. "You mean you didn't know?"

"Didn't know what, Mother?" I throw my hands up in exasperation. "I feel like you are speaking riddles to me."

"Brandon, you're the reason she went to Paris. She was finally going to tell you how she felt, but when she came to tell you, you told her Morgan was pregnant."

My mouth drops open as my mind swims back to that day.

A knock sounds on the door. I was just about to text Presley to ask her over to share the good news, but it can wait. Opening the door, surprise and delight fill me. Presley stands on the other side in a flowered skirt, unusual for her, but I don't ponder the reason for it.

"Presley, I was hoping you'd come by." I grab her hands and pull her into the apartment, shutting the door behind us.

"I have something to tell you." Her words come out as a stutter, again a little odd, but I am so focused on my good news that I pass it off as excitement. Has someone already told her? She and Morgan aren't close, but I suppose it is possible.

I propel her to the hand-me-down couch. As we sit and the rusty springs squeaks, I remember the day we bought it.

At the age of eighteen, I had decided to step out of my father's shadow and his money and try to make it on my own. After I had signed the lease, my first stop had been Presley's. I wanted her help in furnishing the apartment as she was not only my best friend but had a much better aesthetic eye than I did.

Our first stop had been the local Goodwill in the next town for some furniture. This couch was the only one available that day, and though it had a few cringeworthy stains and it wasn't very comfortable, the price tag of twenty dollars had been too good to turn down. We had loaded it, along with another chair and a few tables into the back of my black Chevy truck — the one thing I had kept from my parents.

After another stop at a store for kitchen items, plates, and bedding, we had returned to my new and very empty apartment and set the place up. Hours later, exhausted, we had collapsed for the first time on the couch. The resulting cacophony of squeaks had kept us laughing for a good ten minutes.

As the memory fades, I grab her hands, unable to contain my excitement any longer. "Morgan is pregnant," I say. "I'm going to be a father."

Her mouth drops open, and her eyes blink repeatedly at me. "That's" — the words seem stuck in her throat — "That's wonderful, Brandon."

"I know. I'm so excited. Now, tell me your news."

She swallows and bites the corner of her lip before pasting her own smile. "I'm going to France."

Suddenly the reason for her flowered skirt and stuttering words that I had dismissed as nothing on the day make sense. My mouth parts, and my hand rakes across my beard.

"I didn't know, Mom."

She takes a step toward me and touches my arm. "What happened then is in the past, but you have control over your future."

I nod, but I am more confused than ever now. Should I stop seeing Presley? Should I just be open that I plan on leaving soon? But, she already knows that.

"Come on," my mother says, moving her hand to circle through my arm, "your father needs to walk, and he's being stubborn about it."

She leads me through the living room and into the family room where my father is seated in our large recliner. His bruised eye has faded more today, and he is able to open it completely. The scrapes he received on his head stand out on his bald head, pink reminders of his bad decision. His feet are propped up on the reclining leg bar, and a walker stands to the side.

"Hey, Dad, you ready to go walking?" I force cheeriness I don't feel into my voice; my mind is still focused on Presley.

"No." The word is short and almost snippy. My father, at least before I left, was never grumpy, so it's very different from the man I was used to.

"He's still mad he has to use a walker," my mother explains.

"I don't need it. I just need to walk slower." He crosses his arms and sticks out his bottom lip like a petulant child.

My mother rolls her eyes and shakes her head. "I'll leave you to deal with him." She pats my arm one more time before making her exit.

"Okay Dad, walker or no, let's take a walk."

My father flashes one more pout before closing the footrest and pushing against the chair arms to stand up. His legs wobble beneath him, and I grab his waist before he can fall.

"Dad, there's nothing wrong with needing some help from the walker for a bit. You fell, and you are going to need time to recover."

He glares at me, but finally agrees and takes the walker. It is hard to see him like this, my father who was always so strong now feeble and needing assistance. I think that is part of his reluctance as well; he doesn't want to be weak.

Using the walker, we slowly traverse the house. My father is tired before we have gone completely around the bottom floor. When I deposit him back in the recliner, his breath is labored, and his legs are shaking. I see my week-long trip turning a lot longer.

My phone rings as soon as my father is situated. A quick glance at the caller ID confirms it is my assistant. "Be right back, Dad," I say as I punch the button and head to my room.

"Brandon, how much longer are you going to be gone?" Aubrey's voice is irritated on the other end, and I cringe. It is never a good idea to have Aubrey mad at you. Though usually even keeled, Aubrey is part Irish with fiery red hair and a temper to match.

"My father is worse off than I thought. I'm going to need at least another week, maybe a little longer. Why, what's happening?"

"Stewart is what's happening. He wants to see the presentation. I've told him you need a few more days, but he's getting antsy. He's threatening to go elsewhere if he doesn't see it by Friday."

Cursing the poor timing, I rake a hand through my hair. I've been working on this presentation for a month, and there is no way I'm going to lose it. This could be my ticket to the big leagues and a secure future for Joy. "Okay, I'll book a flight to come home to do the presentation. Just stall him a little longer."

"What do you think I've been doing for the last few days?"

A sigh escapes my lips as I hang up the phone. I'll have to get flowers or something for Aubrey to stay out of the dog house. Standing, I cross to the desk holding my laptop and open the screen. I need to review the presentation and see if it's missing anything.

I'm completely immersed in the slides when my mother enters later, and I jump at the sound of her voice.

"Where's Joy?" she asks. "It's past lunchtime."

My eyes fly to the tiny clock in the bottom right of the computer. Crap. I should have picked her up an hour ago. "She's with Presley." Clicking the save button, I close the screen again. I'll have to finish it later.

"Still?"

"I know Mom, I lost track of time."

Her eyes narrow at me, but before she can give me another lecture, I squeeze past her and down the hall. My coat is on before she enters the living room, and while she says nothing, I can feel her accusing eyes boring into my back. I grab my hat and throw open the door.

The cold blasts my face as I step onto the porch, and I pull my coat tighter. I hadn't even buttoned it up in my haste to exit the house, and I fumble with the buttons now. My breath is creating tiny puffs of smoke as I pick up the pace.

"I'm so sorry," I say, pushing open the door to Presley's shop.

"Daddy," Joy runs to me, throwing her arms about my legs. "We made cookies, and I got to help serve people and then Presley made me lunch on this yummy bread."

As she rattles on, my eyes find Presley. Her head is cocked, and her lips are pursed, not exactly annoyed but I can tell there is something on her mind. My luck with women is zero for two today.

"Thank you," I say, when Joy finishes spilling every minute detail of her morning. Presley nods. "See you tonight?"

She takes a breath as if she wants to say something, but her eyes fall to Joy. "Sure," she says. "Seven?"

I nod. I'll have to pick up flowers for her too.

Chapter Fourteen - Presley

Stepping onto the porch at Brandon's, I am still pondering how to tell him what I want to say. Trudy recommended being blunt, but "Hey, Brandon, your daughter is scared of you because you work so much," just doesn't seem like the right words to say. Nor does, "She stuffed her face with chocolate chips in a cry for attention," but I don't want to be too coy either.

Sighing, I press the doorbell, hoping inspiration will strike me or that God will send me the right words to say. Brandon opens the door and holds out a small bouquet of flowers.

My forehead wrinkles. "What are these for?"

"For helping with Joy today, and for the favor I'm about to ask of you. Can we walk before dinner?"

The air is still cold. Another snow is expected for tonight, but I am bundled up, so I agree. I'm curious as to what this favor entails anyway.

He holds out his arm, and I place mine in his feeling a little like Ginger Rogers with Fred Astaire. "How was the rest of your day?" he asks.

"Fine." My word is slow and cautious as I have no idea what this favor will entail.

He chuckles at my hesitation. "Don't worry, this favor isn't about your job. Well, not really anyway."

My curiosity is piqued more than ever, but I don't ask. He'll tell me when he's ready. "How was your day?" I banter the question back to him in hopes of eliciting more information.

"It was . . . challenging," he says and rubs his free hand over his beard. I don't remember him making this gesture when his face was clean shaven in high school, but it seems to have become a trademark nervous gesture for him. "My dad is still really weak, and he got tired just walking around the house, so I'll probably be staying a little longer than I originally thought."

"Well, that doesn't sound so bad," I said nuzzling into him. It sounded a little like heaven to me, though I didn't know why I was allowing myself to fall for him knowing he planned to leave soon. Did I really think I could get him to stay?

"Yeah, that part's not so bad, but my assistant called and the buyer for this presentation I'm working on wants to see the presentation by Friday."

He pauses as if this should mean something to me, but I have little knowledge of his job and none of this presentation.

"Anyway, it means I need to head back to Dallas for a few days to finish it up, and I know it's a lot to ask, but I was hoping you could help Mom and Anna with Joy. She seems to really like and relate to you."

There it is. My opening. I couldn't have asked for a better lead in. "Of course I will, Brandon, but are you sure you need to do this? I think Joy would benefit more from having you around. She seemed terrified of disappointing you today."

His body stiffens, and he drops my arm. "I'm trying to make the best life I can for Joy, and right now, that means this presentation. Once I get established, then I can worry about spending more time at home."

"But Brandon, what if that takes longer than you think? You remember how hard it was for my brother and me with my mother never around? She only has you, and she needs you."

"Presley, no offense, but you don't know what it's like. Morgan left because we didn't have a stable life, and I don't want Joy to feel the same."

His words hit like a slap in the face. "I may not know your situation exactly, but I know what it's like to be Joy, and I'm telling you she doesn't care about the money; she just wants her daddy home more."

His hand rakes across his beard again. "Let's agree to disagree on this. I don't want to ruin what little time we have left."

Too late. I'm irritated he won't listen to me and annoyed he can't see what he's doing to Joy. The walk back is quiet, strained. Even when the snow starts falling, it doesn't lighten the mood. Instead, it seems to melt before it hits either one of us, as if our tension is creating an unseen heat force.

"Don't say anything about my trip yet," Brandon says as we return to his house. "I haven't told anyone else."

I shake my head. As much as I don't agree, it's not my place to say anything.

As we step inside, the heat rolls over us, and I gratefully peel off my coat and hat. After hanging them on the hat rack, I follow Brandon to the kitchen where everyone is sitting down for dinner.

"Ooh, pretty flowers," Anna says winking at Brandon and smiling at me. If only she knew they were more of a bribe than a token of affection. "Do you want to put them in water?"

I nod, and Anna rifles through a few cabinets until she finds a glass vase. She fills it with water from the tap and places it on the bar. As I unwrap the flowers, my anger dissipates a little. The bright colors of the flowers really are pretty, a combination of red roses, pink carnations, baby's breath, and some purple flower I don't know. He didn't have to buy them for me. He knows I would have helped without the bribe.

"Dinner is served," Beverly says, turning from the stove with a giant pot of spaghetti. Her "kiss the cook" apron is splattered with old stains. I had gotten her the apron the first Christmas I spent with the family because she was always complaining about staining her clothes. I can't believe it's lasted this long.

"Sit by me, Presley," Joy says, grabbing my arm and pulling me to the chair next to hers. Brandon takes her right and Anna takes my left. Bruce is already sitting at the table, but he folds his paper and puts it away. He does still look weak and frail.

Beverly places the pot in the middle of the table before taking her seat. I've always loved her spaghetti. I don't know what she does differently, but something about the meat and sauce combination she uses always makes it taste better.

As she scoots her chair in, we join hands and Bruce prays over the food. In my head, I add a silent prayer for Bruce's health and for Brandon to open his eyes.

"So, I need to head back to Dallas for a few days," Brandon says as he scoops spaghetti on his plate. I'm surprised he brings it up at dinner.

"We're leaving already?" Joy's voice is laced with sadness as she turns her head up to Brandon.

"No, you're staying. Just me. I just need to do a presentation and then I'll be back."

"But why can't you stay?" she asks. "All you ever do is work, and I thought we'd get to spend some time together on this trip."

I shoot a pointed look at Brandon; this is exactly what I had been trying to tell him. The rest of his family is quiet, watching the exchange unfold. An air of tension settles on the table.

"We will spend more time together, but this presentation could lead to a promotion that could set us up for life."

"That's what you always say." Her voice is soft and aimed at her plate. I'm not even sure he heard it, but I did.

"Hey, it's snowing again. Maybe we can build another snowman tomorrow." I nudge her arm and offer a smile, hoping to cheer her up.

She shrugs her small shoulders and twirls her spaghetti. "Okay."

I don't dare look at Brandon again. I might be tempted to shout 'I told you so' at him. The rest of dinner is quiet, as if no one can think of anything to say. Only the sounds of chewing and forks scraping across porcelain plates fills the air.

When dinner ends, Brandon's cell rings and he excuses himself. Joy's eyes are sad as she watches him go. "Hey, do you want to work a puzzle?" I ask her.

She shakes her head. "Nah, that's okay. I'll just go read." Her posture is so dejected as she shuffles to the couch that my heart breaks.

"Why can't he see what he's doing to her?" I ask Beverly and Anna as we clear the plates.

"Because he's stubborn and a man," Anna says.

"Hey, I take offense to that," Bruce says from the end of the table. He's been so quiet that I have forgotten he was even there.

"You're stubborn too," Beverly says pointing her finger at Bruce, "or else you'd be using that walker more."

He crosses his arms and scowls at her, and Beverly turns to me.

"I know it doesn't seem like it now, but he is better around you. I'm hopeful that your influence will show him what really matters." Her eyes are sincere and not pushy.

I sigh. "I tried talking to him today before dinner, but he didn't want to hear it. I'm afraid you might be putting too much stock in his feelings for me."

She places her hand on my arm. "His feelings are deeper than he knows. Give him time."

My eyes wander to Joy, slumped on the couch with a book in her lap. A vein of fear grips my heart as I realize I'm not only falling in love with Brandon, but also with Joy.

Chapter Fifteen - Brandon

"Thank goodness you're here," Aubrey says, accosting me as I enter the office. "Stewart is getting antsy." Her red hair is piled on her head though a few stray hairs have escaped. Her jacket has been removed, displaying a white shell tucked into her blue pencil skirt.

I take a deep breath to keep from snapping at her. I haven't even been home, and I am sticky from the airplane ride. Plus, I'm still recovering from Joy's snub this morning. She wouldn't say goodbye or look me in the eye, and her hug last night had been apathetic as well.

All through the plane ride, Presley's words had haunted my mind. Am I pushing this promotion for the wrong reasons? Maybe I am, but Joy is only five. She doesn't understand the intricacies of life.

I shake my head to clear the invading thoughts away. Once I get this promotion, I'll be able to spend more time with Joy. It will all work out. "Okay," I say, sighing and dropping my overnight bag on the plush tan carpet. "What do we need to do?"

She smiles and motions me to the conference table where she has a laptop set up. "Well, we've set up the preliminary on what the lodge should become, but we need to find pictures to represent what we want, and we need to finish the cost analysis."

My head swims with her onslaught of words, and I rub my hand across my forehead as I sink into one of the chairs. "Right, where are we on the cost analysis anyway?"

"We've figured out how much the renovations will cost, but we need to estimate the return over the next few years."

As the time we'll need adds up in my head, I wonder why I ever thought leaving in the middle of this proposal would be okay. Aubrey and I will have to work nearly non-stop to be ready for Friday. "I'll take the money aspect. Why don't you work on the visual aspect?"

She nods and pivots back to her desk to begin working, and I stare at the screen, willing my mind to focus. Instead, Joy's doe eyes fill my mind. The sight of her sitting on the couch, shoulders slumped papers my vision. I rub my eyes to clear the image. If I can focus, perhaps I can present before Friday and be back sooner.

Two hours later, we call it a day. I need a shower and Aubrey needs to get home to her cat. As I've left my car at my parents' house in Star Lake, Aubrey offers to drive me home and pick me up the next morning.

The apartment is quiet, tomblike, as I enter. It's odd, being here without Joy. Usually, she comes bounding up to me, throws her arms around my legs, and rattles off everything that happened in her day, from what she ate for breakfast to what the characters on her favorite show did. I generally nod, having no idea what she is talking about, but not wanting to let on, and then when I can peel her off, I get a rundown from the nanny, bid her goodnight, and Joy and I sit down to dinner. After dinner, we play for a bit or read and then it's her bath time and bed time. It isn't much time with her during the week, but I always try to make up for the fact on weekends.

I shut the door behind me and lean against it, taking in the apartment. It is eclectic, decorated in whatever I could afford after Morgan left and I had to pay for a nanny and work. The couch is a faded brown squishy thing picked up from Goodwill and scrubbed thoroughly. The pictures on the wall are a mixture of pictures of Joy and odd landscape pictures I picked up from thrift stores. Not exactly my style, but I can't afford the van Gogh's I'd like to own.

Beyond the living room is the kitchen, still glaringly white and green. I've never bothered to paint the walls, but I don't know if it's from lack of time or lack of caring. Dropping my bag onto the kitchen table, I flick the light switch on and open the fridge, hoping for something to jump out at me. I haven't eaten since lunch at the airport, and it wasn't very filling.

Unfortunately, since we've been gone, Amber, the nanny, hasn't been making dinner, so there isn't much to choose from. I resort to an old high school favorite and pull out a few eggs, butter, and the bread.

As I start the eggs cooking, I put the bread in the toaster and wait for it to pop up. A fried egg sandwich is going to feel like a pauper's meal compared to the food my mother has been cooking, but it's better than starving.

When the bread is buttered, and the egg is nestled securely inside, I take out my phone. It's nearly eight but surely Joy will still be awake. My fingers fly across the keys, inputting my mother's number from memory.

She answers on the second ring. "Hey, Mom, can you put Joy on? I want to wish her good night at least."

The pause is so long on the other side that I look at the phone display to make sure it's still connected. "Mom?"

"Hang on. I'm trying to convince her to take your call."

"Daddy?" Joy's voice is not full of the laughter I'm used to. It is quiet and subdued, and it sounds more like a statement than a question.

"Hey, Pumpkin, how was your day?" I try to inject an extra dose of happiness in my voice to try and cheer her up, but it ends up sounding fake even in my ears.

"Fine."

Her monosyllabic words hurt my heart, and I wonder again if I am doing the right thing. I want to hug her and have her tell me about her day, but I can tell she isn't there, so I decide to cut the call short and end both our misery.

"Okay, honey, well, I hope you have a good night, and I'll call again tomorrow."

"Okay."

And then, before I can say goodbye, the line goes dead. I hope my mother is gently informing her that hanging up on her father, even when she is angry, is not the polite thing to do, as I know she would have if it had been me hanging up on my father.

I stare at the phone for a moment and then tap in a different number.

"Hello?"

Presley's voice is a soothing aloe on the other end. I can't believe how quickly she has re-entered and bettered my life. "Hey, Presley. Did you see Joy today?" My finger traces a circle on the dining room table as I wait for her answer.

"Yeah, we built a snowman this afternoon. I closed the shop for a few hours and played with her. She misses you Brandon."

"I know, but I'll be done in a few days, and then I'll be back."

"Until you leave again." Her voice is soft, but there's no denying the sadness in it. I'm not sorry I called, but I do wish the conversations had been happier. After she fills me in on the rest of her day, and I bore her with details of my presentation, we end the conversation.

As I put the phone down, the silence seeps in again, and I wish Presley were here with me. Though hearing her voice helped, I miss her face and her lips. What I wouldn't give to curl up on the couch with her right now and breathe in her scent.

It is still early, but the empty apartment holds nothing for me, so I change into shorts and crawl into bed. I am tired, but Presley's voice reminding me that Joy misses me runs circles through my brain, and doubt that this is the right move creeps in again.

Aubrey arrives at seven the next morning, and after a stop at a coffee shop for a morning pick-me-up, we are back at the office and plugging away.

"Do you think we could finish today?" I ask, lifting the coffee to my mouth. The warm liquid flows down my throat, but it does nothing to ease the ache I feel.

Her green eyes flash at me as she lays her pen down on the table. It is a deliberate controlled movement, and one that shows the anger building inside her. "You want to finish the presentation today?"

Swallowing, I plow ahead, knowing she might blow up at me., "Yes, Aubrey. I miss Joy, and want to spend more time with her while I can. I promised her."

Her eyes bore into mine, but her shoulders relax. Though she doesn't have kids, she has a soft spot for Joy. "Okay, it will mean a busy day today, but I'm almost done with the video aspect if you are close on the cost analysis."

"I am. I think I can finish today."

"Well, we better buckle down then."

She turns the laptop screen toward me and begins the slide show she has assembled. It is good, exciting. I offer a few suggestions and then turn my screen to her, so she can see the cost analysis. She points out a few items I have forgotten, and we dig in and continue working.

When lunch rolls around, she orders in and we keep working. At six pm, we are finished. "Can you call Stewart and ask him to meet us tomorrow instead of Friday?"

She nods and heads over to the phone. I begin practicing the presentation in my head, but I'm not feeling it. I'm worried about Joy, and I want to hear Presley's voice.

"Okay, he can meet us at eight am tomorrow morning," Aubrey says, "and I took the liberty of booking you a return flight for late morning."

"Thank you, Aubrey." She really is an amazing assistant.

I order a pizza after she drops me off and then dial my mother. The phone rings four times before going to the answering machine. My parents have not embraced voice mail and while they each have a cell phone, they almost never answer it.

When the beep sounds, I leave a message, trying to sound cheerful, though loneliness is all I feel. "Hi guys. I hope everyone is well. I'm almost finished here and should be home tomorrow. I can't wait to see you, Joy. I miss you."

I end that call and dial Presley's number. Chances are she is with them wherever they are.

"Hi, you've reached Presley, but I can't answer the phone right now. Leave a message at the beep."

My heart aches even more at the sound of her sweet voice and the fact it's only her recording. I hang up without leaving a message. Not talking to them compounds the loneliness, but perhaps it will allow me to focus on practicing for the presentation.

Chapter Sixteen - Presley

"What do you want to do today?" I ask Joy. I've shut the shop down early again to have some time to spend with her. I'm hopeful my customers will be understanding; I can't really afford to lose any business right now.

"Can we build another snowman?" Her eyes dance at the prospect, and she folds her hands together in a pleading gesture. Her lip falls out in a perfect pout, a trait she must have gotten from Brandon as he too had perfected the gesture on me in high school.

I look out into the backyard, but we used most of its snow yesterday and Sunday, and there hasn't been any new snowfall.

"How about we go to the lake and see if there's enough there to build a snowman."

"Yes." The word is squealed in delight, and she bounds off to get her coat and hat.

"You want to come, Anna?"

Anna and Beverly both sit at the kitchen table. Beverly is working a book of crossword puzzles, and Anna is reading a book.

"Sure," she sighs. "This isn't catching my interest much anyway." She closes the book and pushes back her chair.

After bundling up, we step out into the cold air and begin the short trek to the lake. Joy runs ahead of us, stopping every now and then to pick up a stick or a stray leaf. The snow is thinner here on the sidewalks due to the foot traffic.

I shove my hands in my pockets and voice the words that have been parading through my head. "Do you think he'll ever stay here?" I ask Anna, my words punctuated with little bits of smoke.

She shrugs and sighs. "I don't know, Presley. Morgan really did a number on him. I think his avoidance of this place has more to do with her than with the place itself."

It is what I expected, but it doesn't make me feel any better.

"Do you think you would ever move to be with him? I know Joy has really taken to you. She could use a good mother figure."

It was my turn to sigh. "I'm not sure. I love Joy, and care deeply for Brandon, but I did the big city in Paris, and it wasn't all I thought it would be. There's something about a small town where everyone knows you that is welcoming."

"Yeah, I missed that this year." Her head drops, and her eyes focus on the ground. Her shoulders roll forward from the invisible weight she is carrying on them.

"What happened, Anna?"

"Nothing, really, but it was so big that I didn't make any close friends. It just felt lonely, and after being here — well it was a shock."

I can relate to her feelings. Being more of an introvert myself, the move to Paris had been a shock, and if it hadn't have been for Pierre — as much as I loathed him cheating on me at the end — I don't think I would have lasted as long as I did. Anna isn't as quiet as I am, but I can imagine the shock of a big college campus. "Will you go back?" We have reached the lake, and she and I sit down on the green park bench.

She plucks a leaf off a bust that sits next to the bench. "I don't know. I do want to get my nursing degree, but I might consider a closer school for next year. My dad falling really affected me too. They are both getting older, and I want to be closer to them in case something happens again."

I can relate to that. My mother and Ryan are all I have, and even though I live in an apartment attached to my mother's house, I rarely see her, but at least I would be close by if anything happened.

"Presley?"

The male voice grabs my attention, and for a moment my heart believes it is Brandon, but as I turn to the approaching figure, the proportions are not right to be Brandon. The figure is taller and a little thicker. "Ryan?" I jump up from the bench and run to embrace my brother. He graduated from college this last summer, but I haven't seen him since then. He's been working as an architect in a firm in Houston.

He picks me up and twirls me around. Even though he's younger, he has always been bigger than I am, at least since he turned thirteen and shot up like a weed. "What are you doing here?"

"I came to spend Christmas with my mom and sister. I took a week off work."

"But how did you know where to find me?"

He rolls his eyes. "I was accosted by Paula on my way in. She told me you had been hanging out with Brandon Scott and that if I couldn't find you at the bakery, then to check his house." He shuddered and rubbed his arms. "I wish she would just use words and not her hands so much."

I laugh as the mental picture appears in my mind. I can almost see Paula's hand gliding up Ryan's muscular arm as she shares her gossip.

"When did you start hanging out with Brandon again? I thought that was over."

I shake my head. "It's a long story."

Ryan's eyes shift from my face to something over my right shoulder. I turn to see Anna approaching us.

"Anna Scott?"

"Hi Ryan. You look good." Anna's hands are clasped in front of her, and as she twirls the ring on her right hand, I remember Ryan telling me they had dated for a little bit in high school, after my move to Paris.

I give him a nod in her direction and step back to the bench.

"Can we build the snowman now?" Joy asks as she runs up to the bench. I have forgotten that was our purpose in coming here, but I smile and start rolling snow for her.

Ryan and Anna soon join in, and between the three of us, we manage to put together a snowman taller than me. In fact, he is almost Ryan's height. Joy scurries toward the lake and returns with two sticks for arms and two rocks for eyes. Ryan lifts her up so she can place the eyes herself.

"It's too bad we didn't bring a carrot," she says, stepping back and admiring our work after Ryan returns her to the ground.

"I think he looks wonderful anyway," I say.

"I agree," Anna says, smiling shyly at Ryan. "I know, who's up for a movie? I think they are playing a Christmas movie."

"Me, me, I love movies," Joy says jumping up and down.

I shrug. "Fine with me. I have nothing better to do." My phone has been too silent all day.

"Ryan?"

He shrugs as well. "Sure, I love a good Christmas movie, but can we get something to eat first? I'm starving."

At the words, my stomach joins in with a rumbling chorus. "Alright, to Max's."

Joy and I lead the way, so Anna and Ryan can have a little privacy behind us. The Diner is busier than I have seen it in a while, and we have to squeeze into a small table near the kitchen.

Max drops off menus without a word as he maneuvers plates of food to another table. After placing their plates down, he comes back our direction.

"What'll you have?"

"What's going on Max? Why is it so busy?"

He rolls his eyes. "Barnard thought it would be a good idea to drum up business for the local shops by offering sales. Today is evidently half price burger day. Course he never told me about it." Max raises his voice and glares across the room. I look to see Barnard wave before shoving a burger in his mouth.

"Oh dear, I better find out what he has planned for me. I'll take a burger by the way." As Max finishes taking orders, I ease out of my chair and finagle through the crowded chairs to Barnard. "What is going to be the sale at the bakery? I need to have some warning as I'm helping out with Joy while Brandon is gone."

He motions me to lean down. "There is no sale for the other businesses. I just wanted a half price burger today, but maybe it's not a bad idea looking at this crowd, huh?"

I shake my head at Barnard. The man certainly has guts. He better hope Max never finds out, or I can't imagine what will happen.

"So, what does he have planned for you?" Ryan asks as I return to the table.

"Nothing," I say quietly. "He just wanted a half price burger."

Anna and Ryan stifle their laughter as Max returns with our drinks.

"What's so funny?" he asks, eying us.

"Nothing, nothing at all," I say, shaking my head before another giggle takes over.

"Barnard!" Max's voice has turned from frustration into an angry growl as he marches over to Barnard, who pales, shrinks, then turns red and puffs up. Max leads Barnard out of the building and the two proceed to have an angry spat in front of the store. We can't hear their words, but their angry gesticulations say a lot.

"I would not want to be Barnard right now," Ryan says, whistling through his teeth.

Moments later, the two return. Max stomps into the kitchen and Barnard stops at the door and raises his hands. "Excuse me, folks, can I get your attention. I'm afraid there was a mix up and there is no half price burger day."

The crowd groans and boos.

"But, but," he continues, "to make up for it, I am offering a free scoop of ice cream to everyone in this restaurant." The words look as if they physically pain him to say.

"Score one for Max," I whisper as the crowd grumbles and returns to their food.

Max appears a moment later and plops our plates down on the table. He may have won, but it did nothing to soften his mood.

After the food is finished and the tab is paid, we head down the street to the cinema. Miracle on 34th Street is playing, and after purchasing tickets, we head into the one theater. The chairs are old and worn, a faded brown from the eighties and patched in many places, but they work. A few other people are in the theater, but we have our choice of seats. Joy leads us down the aisle to about ten rows from the screen and smack dab in the middle of the row. It's closer than I usually sit, but I don't have to crane my neck, so I agree. Anna sits next to me and Ryan on the other side of her. I somehow doubt either one of them will really be paying close attention to the movie.

When I return home from watching the movie with Joy, Anna and Ryan, I see a missed call from Brandon on my cell phone. I click on the voicemail button, but there is nothing waiting. Why didn't he leave a message?

I consider calling him back, but it is nearly ten. If he is working, I don't want to bother him, and if he's sleeping, I don't want to wake him. Perhaps it is better this way anyway. If he still plans on leaving, I should probably begin distancing myself, if that is even possible.

An exasperated sigh escapes my lips, and Niko looks up from his dish on the counter where he has been crunching his dry cat food.

"I don't know what I'm doing Niko. I'm just going to get my heart broken again."

Niko wanders over to me and rubs against my hand. At least he understands; he always understands.

Flicking off the kitchen light, I head down the hall to my bedroom. It's late and five am comes early. The nice thing about owning my own store is being able to set my hours, but owning a cupcake shop/bakery means people expect to get their breakfasts there, which means opening by seven am.

Changing into shorts and a tank top, I wonder if I could move with him. Could I close the shop and reopen somewhere with him if he asked me to? I find no easy answer as I brush my teeth and climb into bed, so I hand it over to the Lord in prayer.

The next morning, the answer is no clearer, but I have faith that he will show me the answer when he's ready.

The day is slow, and I find myself whipping out my cell phone between customers to check for a message from Brandon, but it is always empty.

After the lunch rush, I take out a rag and begin wiping down the tables. The bell jingles and Joy comes rushing in.

"Presley, did you hear? Daddy's coming back tonight."

"Sorry, she just had to tell you," Anna says, shaking her head.

"That's okay," I say to her before turning my attention to Joy, who is patting my hip excitedly. "No, I hadn't heard, but I didn't get to talk to your daddy last night. That is good news though." Why hadn't he left a message telling me that? The thought sends tiny tendrils of doubt mixing with the happiness at seeing him again.

"He said he'd be home tonight. You'll come, won't you?"

"Of course I will." Though I wonder if the reason he didn't tell me he was coming home is because he didn't want me there. Joy hugs my legs before dashing over to the pastry case and pressing her nose and hands against the freshly wiped glass.

"Dinner will be at seven," Anna says. "Will that give you enough time?"

"Yeah, it gives me plenty of time." I had tried staying open later than six in case people wanted dessert after dinner, but very few people had shown up, so I had left the hours from seven to six, which gave me some time to myself in the evenings.

"Great, we'll see you then. We have to go expend some energy." She nods at Joy, who is tapping at the glass as if trying to convince the pastries to come out. "Come on, Joy. Let's let Presley get back to work."

Joy smiles and waves as she bounds out of the shop, and I return to wiping tables. I've just finished re-wiping the glass case when the bell sounds again and Paula saunters in, a black knit dress clinging to her large frame. A white fur coat covers most of her top half.

"Well, hello Paula, what can I get for you today?"

Her bright red lips purse as she peruses the offerings in the case. "I'll have that." She points an equally red fingernail at a mini chocolate pie, and I bend down to snag it from the case. "Where is that handsome man of yours?" she asks, peering behind the counter in hopes of finding him stashed back there.

"He had to take a trip back to his job, but he'll be back soon." I place the pie in a little brown box and begin closing the flaps.

"It's not another woman, is it?" Her voice is low and conspiratorial as if we are sharing a secret. I don't bite.

"No, just work, Paula. Here you go. That will be two fifty."

She hands over the money, looking disappointed that I didn't have any more gossip to share with her.

At six pm, I bundle up, lock the door, and head home to change. My stomach is a wad of knots at seeing Brandon again and hearing how his presentation went. I don't want to hope it didn't go well, but I can't stop the thought.

Changing into a blue sweater that brings out my eyes, I run a brush through my hair, check Niko's food and water, and then head back out into the cold.

Chapter Seventeen - Brandon

As the taxi pulls up to the house, I take a deep breath before throwing open the door. This is not going to be easy, and though I've been practicing the words to say the whole way here, nothing sounds right.

The driver pops the trunk, and I remove my bag and place a tip in his hand. He taps his head and gets back in the car, leaving me staring at the house.

Another deep breath gives me the strength to climb the first step. The door is unlocked, and I enter quietly, hoping to surprise Joy. Somehow, I doubt she will be enthused by my news, and I'd like to see her happy for a moment before facing the tears I know will come.

Noise from the kitchen draws me that direction, and I turn the corner to see my entire family, Presley included, gathered around the table. The happy picture strikes me, and I wonder again if I am making the right decision.

"Daddy." Joy sees me first and scrambles off her chair. Her hug is so forceful it sends me back a step.

"Hi, Pumpkin. I missed you too." I bend down to give her a proper hug. My eye catches Presley's over Joy's shoulder, and she smiles and flicks a small wave.

"How was your trip?" My mother asks.

It's my opening, but I am too scared to take it right now. I'll save my news for later. "It was good, but I am famished. There was no food in my place, well no real food anyway. Please tell me you're cooking something amazing."

"Roast and potatoes and salad."

My mouth waters at the words and the scent of roasting meat I can now smell. Joy tugs my hand to the table, and as I sit, she tells me everything they did over the last two days. Presley takes the chair to my left, and her hand finds mine under the table and squeezes. I hope she will feel the same way after she hears my news.

After dinner, I decide the news can't wait any longer. "Can everyone join me in the living room?" Their faces are a series of questions, but everyone heads that direction. My father even uses his walker, which helps me feel a little better about leaving.

"So, you guys all know that I was doing this presentation the last few days. Stewart really liked it, and he offered me a job working for his company."

"That's wonderful," my mother says, but her voice relays her true feelings. She doesn't find it wonderful at all.

"Where is the job?" Presley's voice is soft, and her blue eyes are filled with sadness as they meet mine.

"New York."

"Where's New York?" Joy asks. The somber mood has hit her, and her voice is full of fear.

"It's up north, honey, but it will be fun. We'll get to live in a big building, and they have lots of fun places to see."

"I don't wanna go." She crosses her arms and stomps her foot. "I wanna stay here with family and with Presley. I like it here." This is exactly the reaction I was expecting.

"I know you do, bug, but this is a great opportunity for Daddy. One that will set us up for a good life."

"It's always about you," she says, water filling up her eyes. "How come you never ask me what I want?"

"Because I'm trying to do what's best for both of us."

"No, you're doing what's best for you, like you always do," she says. "I hate you, and I don't want to go." With that she runs out of the room. My mother rises to go after her, but I hold up my hand.

"Just let her go. She needs to cool off a little." The tension in the room presses down on all of us, and I shift uncomfortably in my chair. I knew this would be hard, but I had been hoping for some happiness or heartfelt congratulations at least.

"When do you leave?" Presley asks.

"Next Friday." There is so much more I want to say to her. I want to ask her to come with me, but it will have to wait until we can be alone.

"You're leaving before Christmas?" This time the shocked voice is my mother's.

"I know the timing is bad, but Dad is looking better, and I pushed for as late as I could." I had tried to push the start date back to the New Year, but Stewart was adamant he wanted me in place before the end of the year.

"I can't believe you, Brandon. The one Christmas we would get to spend with our granddaughter and you leave early. Have you even thought about how much this will upset her?"

My anger boils over, and I lash out at my mother. "Of course I have, Mom. I tried to push it back, but this is a once in a lifetime opportunity, and I can't let it pass me. I'll finally get to have everything you and Dad did before you moved here."

My mother's jaw drops open, and my father, who has been sitting quietly, clears his throat. "Do you not remember why we moved here, Brandon?"

"You retired, and we needed a smaller place."

He shakes his head. "No, I retired because I didn't like what the money was doing to us. Your mother was hung up on all the latest fashions and spending more on shoes than food each month. You and Anna were quickly following in her footsteps. I didn't want to lose my family to money, so I took an early retirement and moved us here, so we could start over and focus on what really matters."

"I won't get like that again Dad. I know how to avoid it now, but I need to do this for Joy."

"For Joy or for you?" His face is as serious as his voice, and he locks eyes with me. I tell myself it is for Joy, but as I hold his stare, I begin to wonder again.

"Well, this sounds like a family affair, so I think I'll be going," Presley says, rising from the couch.

"Wait, Presley, I need to talk with you. Let me walk you home." She shrugs but does not say no, and I take that as a yes.

When we step outside, I reach for her hand, and while she allows me to hold it, she does not return the grip. "Presley, I want you to come with me. I can't imagine going without you, and Joy adores you. You always talked about working in a big city. You could open a shop there and live your dream too."

Her shoulders rise with the breath she takes. "I have a life here, Brandon, and my own shop. I'll have to think about it."

It is not the answer I had hoped for, but it isn't a firm no, which gives me hope. "Please do." When we arrive at her doorstep, I lean in to kiss her, but she turns her head, and my lips land on her cheek.

"Just give me time," she says, and before I can say anything else, she has entered her apartment and shut the door. I stand staring at the white door and wondering how everything got so messy.

Chapter Eighteen ~ Presley

After Brandon leaves, I enter the main house, looking for Ryan. He's not normally my confidant, but I need to process. He is parked in front of the TV watching sports.

"Can you turn that off a moment?"

Without questioning, he flicks the remote and turns his attention to me. He will make some woman very happy one day. I sit down on the other side of the couch from him.

"Brandon just told us he's taking a job in New York, and he wants me to go with him."

His eyebrow inches up his forehead. "Are you going to go?"

"That's the thing, I don't know." I grab a piece of hair and twirl it in my fingers. "I want to be with him, but I like it here. I like the slower pace and the people are friendly. Weird, but friendly. It's home, you know?"

"I do now," he says, nodding. "I've been thinking about coming back myself."

"Before or after you saw Anna?" I say, punching his leg.

"Before," he smiles, "but I certainly wouldn't say no to being closer to Anna."

"Why did the two of you break up anyway?"

He shakes his head. "I don't even remember. Something stupid would be my guess. That's usually why people break up. I haven't seen you with Brandon, but I know how much you cared about him in high school. Are you sure you want to lose that?"

I shake my head. I'm not sure of anything except how unsure of everything I am. "Thanks, Ryan. I guess I have some thinking to do."

"And some praying." He rises from the
 couch with me and gives me a hug before flicking the remote back on.

I walk back to my apartment, my brain even more confused than when I came over. With a sigh, I get ready for bed, hoping that everything will be clearer in the morning. Crawling into bed, I give it over to God.

The next morning, Paula is waiting outside the door to my shop when I arrive.

"Am I late, Paula?" I check my watch, but it shows five till seven.

"No, I just wanted to see how you were doing. I heard Brandon is moving to New York."

I blink at her. I have no idea how she heard that information so quickly; she's like some kind of super magnet for gossip. "He is, but I'm fine. Thank you for asking." I shoulder past her to insert the key in the door.

She follows me inside. "Not that we want you to leave, but are you thinking about going with him?" She's fishing now; maybe this is how she gets her information.

"I don't know, Paula. I haven't decided." I flick the lights on and head to the back.

"Oh, well, while I'm here, perhaps I'll see what you are offering today." She sidles up to the counter.

"Right, give me a second." I hurry into the back and grab the left-over pastries. She waits patiently while I unwrap them and place them on the trays. I'll have to do some cooking today as the inventory is running low.

She selects her pastries and waves goodbye. After the door closes, I head to the back to grab the ingredients I need to make some new desserts. I spend the day whipping up new batches of muffins, brownies, and cookies in between the customers that walk in the door, asking the same questions that Paula did. By the time it is closing time, I am exhausted both from cooking and from answering questions, but I finally have my answer.

I nearly lose my nerve as I step onto Brandon's porch, but it must be done. My breath comes out in a giant sigh as I press the doorbell. Brandon opens the door, and his eyes so full of hope nearly change my mind.

"I was hoping you would come by tonight," he says, opening the door for me to come in. He leans in to kiss me, and because I know it will probably be the last one, I savor the feel of his lips on mine.

I must have done something differently because I can see in his eyes when he pulls back that he knows something is off. "Can we talk somewhere?"

He nods, and taking my hand, leads me to his room. As the door shuts, I take a deep breath. "Brandon, I adore you and Joy, but I realized today that I love this town and the people in this town. I've never been to New York, but if it's like Paris, you don't get customers like that, people who care about you and come in to ask you how you are."

"Maybe it will be different than Paris," he says, and the hope in his voice pulls at my heart.

"I can't go, Brandon. It's not just that. You are different when you work that job. You're so relaxed and kind here, but whenever your phone rings, you change. You become this stiff, focused, almost angry man, and I wouldn't be able to bear seeing you like that every day. I would resent you and the move. It wouldn't be good for anyone."

I can tell I've struck a nerve as he bristles and takes a step away from me. "Fine, Presley. I shouldn't have asked you to come anyway, but I thought you wanted a chance to realize your dream."

"I'd like to say goodbye to Joy, and then I think it would be best if I don't come back before you leave. I don't want to make it any harder on Joy." The words scrape like a razor blade against my heart as they pour out of my mouth.

"That's probably best."

There is a wall between us now, an invisible field of tension that pulls at my heart. This is not the way I wanted it to go at all. Nodding, I open the door and head down the hallway to the living room. The family is gathered there watching a movie. Joy looks up at the sound of my footstep and comes running. I catch her in a hug, and the tears I have been holding back so well threaten to pour down my cheeks.

"Presley, I wondered when you would get here. Come watch with us." She begins to tug at my hand in an effort to lead me to the couch.

"I can't, Joy. I came to say good bye."

"Good bye? Where are you going?" Her face scrunches in confusion.

"I'm not going anywhere, honey, but I'm not coming to New York with you either, and since I'm not," *and since Brandon and I just broke up, I think*, "I thought it would be best if I didn't come back around. I don't want to make it harder on you when it's time to go."

Her blue eyes begin to shimmer as they fill with tears. "No, you have to keep coming, Presley. I don't want you not to come back."

"I know, Joy, but one day, I think you'll thank me for this."

She throws her arms around me one more time and sobs into my shoulder. The sound breaks the last wall I had built around my heart and my tears join hers. When she pulls back, she flashes her eyes at Brandon. "This is your fault," she says. "I hate this move, and

I hate you." As she runs from the room, the rest of us stare after her, unsure what to say or do.

The uncomfortable weight settles on my shoulders, and I stand, wiping the tears from my eyes. "Bruce, I'm glad to see you improving. Beverly, thank you for a wonderful few weeks. Anna, I'm sure I'll be seeing more of you." I turn to Brandon who is leaning against the wall with his arms crossed. "Brandon, I . . ." I want to tell him I love him, but this doesn't seem the time or the place. "I had a wonderful time, and I will miss you incredibly. Most of all, I'm sorry."

He says nothing, but his hand rubs his beard again, and his eyes pull up to the right. I can tell he is fighting emotion too. Before, I become a blubbering mess, I exit the room and show myself out of the house. The tears hit with full force as the front door closes behind me, and a loud sob escapes my lips. Pain like I've never felt before rips through my body, shattering my heart into a million pieces. Head down, I hurry home and throw myself onto my bed. Niko jumps up beside me, but even his purring and butting me with his head can't change my mood. I feel broken and empty and immediately wonder if I've made the right decision.

Chapter Nineteen - Brandon

The taxi pulls up in front of the high-rise apartment building, and Joy's eyes widen. "We're going to live here?"

"Only for a month or so. The company is putting us up in their suite until we decide where we want to live." Though she's not entirely on board, it is good to see Joy finding some happiness in the move. Leaving the family had certainly been tough.

The day Presley said she wasn't coming had been the worst. I had expected she wouldn't leave, Star Lake was her home and she fit there, but actually hearing the words had created a pain I didn't know could exist. Joy had taken it even harder, clinging to Presley and then spewing hatred at me. She had spent the rest of the day in her room, not even coming out for meals.

I couldn't fault Presley. I knew she was trying to make it easier on Joy, but it sure had been harder the next few days. Joy had been nearly mute, only answering when directly spoken to. Even on the airplane ride here, which she normally loved, she had been stony silent.

The company had offered to pack up my apartment and ship the car, and I had taken them up on it, so Joy and I had only packed a few changes of clothes and her favorite toys of course.

As Joy steps onto the sidewalk, her head goes from one high rise to the next. Her mouth is open in a nearly perfect "oh" shape. I grab our bags from the trunk and tip the driver. The taxi pulls away from the curb and joins the flood of traffic. I want to hold Joy's hand, but my arms are full of the luggage.

"Come on, grab my pocket," I say. The crowd is much larger here, and my fear of losing Joy in a car accident is quickly being replaced by her being abducted or shuffled away in the throng of busy New Yorkers who have their phone attached to their ears and their eyes on their watches. I'd forgotten how impersonal busy executives can be.

The door of the apartment building opens as we approach, and a man in a maroon suit greets us. "Welcome to the Stratton apartments. Please come in." After a little perfunctory bow, he spans his arm out and steps back, holding the door open and allowing our entrance.

The lobby of the apartment is like an expensive hotel, decorated in reds and golds. My eyes are nearly as wide as Joy's as I take in the opulence. Large, golden chandeliers hang from gold-plated ceilings, creating a stunning visual display. Four red couches create a large square around a glass-topped coffee table. An enormous white marble desk occupies the right corner, a colorless distraction from the stimulating room.

A petite brunette with her hair pulled tightly on her head mans the counter. I sidle her direction, making sure Joy is still firmly grasping my pocket.

"Hi, I'm Brandon Scott. Stewart said to check in with you. We'll be staying in the company suite."

Her head nods, just once, proficiently. "Absolutely, Mr. Scott." She punches the keys on her computer. "There you are. I just need you to sign this. It's a listing of the rules and the responsibility clause."

A printer whirs to life behind her, and she turns, grabs the sheet, and places it before me. It reads like a small contract. No loud noise after eight pm, all visitors after six pm must be approved by the front desk, no pets – good thing we don't have any. Nothing seems out of order, so I initial and sign at the bottom before handing it back to her.

Her eyes scan the paper. "Very good, sir. One moment."

As she reaches for the phone beside her, I glance down at Joy. Her eyes are still wide, and her hands clutch her bunny in a death grip.

"Don't worry, Bug, it gets easier once you get used to it."

A moment later, another man in a maroon suit appears at our side. His nose is long and hawkish above a neatly trimmed brown mustache that matches his eyebrows and the sideburns peeking out from under his hat.

"I'll take those, Sir, and show you to your apartment."

Grateful, I hand over two of the bags, keeping my laptop bag over my shoulder. With my now free hand, I grasp Joy's and we follow the man whose name tag read Mark. He leads us down a marble floored hallway where the red and gold décor follow. Elegant abstract paintings are hung at interspersed intervals along the wall.

Mark stops in front of an elevator with ornate gold doors. The button chimes and lights up as his finger presses it. Instead of the normal digital display of floors, there is an old timey arc of numbers and an arrow that points to each one as it passes that floor.

When the arrow touches down on the number one, the elevator dings and the door slides open. The inside has a gold and white interior and a dark red carpet. A golden panel with rows of buttons from one to thirty lines one side, and as we step in, Mark punches button thirty.

The doors close, and the elevator ascends, but the movement is so smooth it is barely noticeable. At the top of the doors is the little black panel that illuminates the number of each floor as we pass. When the elevator hits thirty, another chime sounds, and the doors open.

The deep red carpet carries into the hallway. Mark turns to the right and leads us to the single white door at the end. As he slides the key into the door, I look behind us. There is only one other door on this floor at the other end of the hallway.

"Who lives in the other apartment?" I ask, hoping it is perhaps a large family with children for Joy to play with.

"The head of the company." Mark's reply is short and succinct. I will be getting no more information from him.

He swings open the door to our apartment, and my jaw drops. The place is huge. A wall of windows faces us, staring into the heart of New York. Two plush leather couches face a giant television mounted on the wall. To the left is a kitchen and dining room done all in black and white.

"The bedrooms are to the right. There are four, so you have your choice. Does it meet your approval?"

I can only nod, awestruck by the immensity of the apartment. I knew the company had money, but I wasn't expecting anything this extreme.

Mark sets down our suitcases and stands patiently waiting. I cock my head at him before it dawns on me that he is waiting for a tip. After extricating my wallet, I hand him two bills, and he nods and exits the room.

"Shall we go pick our rooms?" I ask Joy.

"It's so big." Her voice tremors with fear. This place must seem even larger to her. My apartment back in Dallas had been a modest two-bedroom. Nothing fancy, but enough for the two of us.

"It will be okay. It's only for a little bit. When we get our new place, it will be much smaller." Even on my new larger salary, I will never be able to afford a place like this.

The floors in the apartment are hardwood, and our feet plop softly on the wood as we head down the hallway. The first room on the right opens to a large guest bathroom decorated in beige and crème. Across from it is the first bedroom, which holds a full bed, dresser, and small desk. The room is blue and white.

The next door reveals a similar room only done in pink and white, and the third door opens to a crème and beige one. At the end of the hall is the last door. I assume it is the master bedroom.

It opens to reveal an enormous room with a king canopied bed. A rose-colored lounging couch sits near the window. A massive maple dresser fills the wall across from the bed and above it is another massive television. A large roll-top desk fills another corner next to a door I am sure leads to the bathroom and closets.

"Can I just sleep in here with you?" Joy asks. "You can lay a mattress on the floor."

"For tonight," I say and pat her head. "We'll see if we can get a smaller bed for the pink room tomorrow if you think that one's too big."

The next morning, I roll over to find Joy curled up in the bed beside me, bunny snuggled under her chin. Her little pink lips are slightly parted, and a soft snore escapes her lips with each breath.

Quietly, I crawl out of the bed and pad to the kitchen to start some coffee. The hardwood floors are cold in the morning, sending a shiver through my body, even though I'm relatively warm in my flannel pants and t-shirt.

I begin opening random cabinets in search of coffee mugs and grounds. The first cabinet reveals plates and bowls, all solid black. The second holds glasses of all kinds. The third cabinet reveals mugs, and I grab a black one with the words "I need a coffee break" emblazoned in white lettering across it.

Mug in hand, I scan the room for a pantry. That's where I would keep coffee. Two white recessed doors catch my eye, and upon opening them, I find a completely stocked pantry with cereal boxes, canned goods, and coffee.

After grabbing the grounds and a filter, I set the coffee pot up and press the button to start brewing. The small machine whirs to life with a few clicks, and the smell of coffee begins to fill the air, followed by the soft dripping of liquid magic into the mug.

When the final hiss ends, I grab the mug and look up to see Joy standing at the end of the bar. Her eyes are still heavy with sleep.

"Hey, Pumpkin. Do you want some cereal? I saw some in the pantry. The good kind." I wiggle my eyebrows at her in hopes of earning a smile.

"Okay," she says. Not quite the reaction I was hoping for, but I grab her a bowl and fill it up with one of the sugary cereals and place it on the table in front of her.

The doorbell rings as I'm replacing the milk in the also well-stocked refrigerator. My brows knit together as I wonder who could be on the other side. Almost no one knows we're here besides Stewart, and he agreed to give me a few days to find a nanny for Joy before calling me into work.

"Stay here, Bug," I say to Joy as I head to the door. My eyes glance around for anything I could use as a weapon, but while this apartment is fully stocked, there is no baseball bat or crow bar lying around anywhere.

At the door, I peer through the peephole and my heart stops. It can't be. I can't keep the trembling from my fingers as I turn the lock on the door.

Chapter Twenty - Presley

*T*hough the sun is shining brightly through the pale curtains covering the window, it does not bring cheer. It's been nearly a week since the last time I saw Brandon and Joy, and my mood has been sour every day.

I kick back the covers and stumble to the shower. Even the warm water and lavender scented soap, which usually awaken my senses, make no dent on my mood today. I grab a pair of pants and a shirt from the closet without even looking to see if they match and then saunter into the kitchen for some coffee.

Twenty minutes later, I am opening the bakery, oblivious to the white wonderland that still covers the town. As the door closes and I flip the sign to open, I force a smile to my face. I refuse to lose my customers simply because I am heartbroken over a boy yet again.

I rescue the left-over pastries from the freezer and begin heating them up. My stomach grumbles at the smell, and I realize I have forgotten to eat or maybe I skipped it on purpose. Food holds no flavor lately.

The bell jingles, and I greet my first customer of the day. Though not a heavy onslaught, the customers continue steadily for the next few hours.

After the breakfast rush and another grumble from my stomach, I take a break and nibble a scone. When the bell jingles, I nearly drop it until I realize it is just Trudy.

"Sit down and take a break like a normal person," she says in her no-nonsense voice. Her finger wags at me with each word. "Stop hiding in the corner, sneaking food. It makes you seem like you're doing something wrong."

Trudy has this brusque way about her that I love, but it also makes me feel sheepish sometimes. Pastry in hand, I walk out from behind the counter and join her at a table. She's in her overalls but free from paint.

"Are you not painting today?" I ask before taking a bite of the scone. The hungry monster in my stomach demands more, and I force my hand to the table to stop it from shoving the entire pastry in my mouth.

"Not yet. I had to check in on my grandmother." Trudy's grandmother lives in the Star Lake nursing home on the outskirts of town. I've never met her grandmother, but Trudy has told me stories. She sounded like an amazing and interesting woman until dementia set in. Now, it seems she hardly even remembers Trudy.

"How is she doing?"

Trudy shrugs, and her eyes drop to the tabletop. "She's okay, I guess. She knew me for a bit today, and she kept asking about Jacob. He was her husband, but he died ages ago. It got me thinking though." Her brown eyes pull back up to mine. "Maybe there is something to this love thing."

My head drops forward in surprise, and I nearly choke on the morsel in my mouth. "Trudy, are you going soft on me?"

Her face scrunches in alarm. "No, not for me. I'm too set in my ways. I mean for you. You and Brandon. The two of you could have a love like my Bethel and Jacob did. I saw it in the way you looked at each other."

"I don't know," I say, shaking my head. "He took the job and moved to New York. He asked me to go with him, but I just couldn't do it. My home is here, and it didn't go well the last time I saw him."

Her hand reaches across the table and grabs my arm. It is two shades darker than mine due to Trudy's ability to tan every time she is in the sun. I envy that about her. I am the type of person who burns and then peels, no matter how much sun I get.

"I don't want you to go," she says, "but what if this is a once in a lifetime love? Would you give that up just to stay here in Podunk Star Lake?"

"I like it here." She shoots me a pointed stare. "Okay, I've been praying about what to do, but my last venture into the big city didn't go so well. Remember?"

She flicks her hand and leans back, dismissing my concern. "Yeah, but that wasn't with Brandon. You know him. Would he do that?"

I want to say no, but he has changed some since I knew him well in high school, and I am no longer confident in my answer. The Brandon I knew hadn't been so obsessed with money, and I'd like to think he would have stayed where his daughter was most comfortable. I certainly can't imagine the Brandon from high school dragging her off to a big city where she knows no one right before Christmas.

The image of Joy clinging to my neck as we said goodbye still pulls on my heartstrings, and I'm no longer sure whether I love her or Brandon more.

"Why don't you at least go visit? Check out the place and see if you could live there?" Trudy glances at her watch. "Plus, if you hurry, you could get there by Christmas."

I gesture at the empty store. "Who would run the store? I can't just close it for a week."

Trudy tips her head to the side. "You could. In this town, it would be fine, but what if I run it for you?"

"You? You hate even helping me clean." Who is this woman in front of me?

She nods. "I do, but I love you, and want the best for you."

I stare at her, trying to decide if she's serious and if I could take her up on it. It would only be for a few days, and it would be nice to spend Christmas with Joy. I know she was upset having to leave and with a new job, Brandon is probably distracted, but do I want to butt in her life again if I'm not going to stay? I don't want to make it harder on the poor girl.

"I'll think about it," I tell Trudy, but in my mind, I'm already packing my bags.

Chapter Twenty-One - Brandon

I had thought I was imagining things, but as the door opens, it is clear the woman in front of me is indeed Morgan. Her face hasn't aged a day. It is still chiseled to perfection with high cheekbones, a classic upturned nose, and flawless skin. Her dark hair cascades around her shoulders, which are hidden under a tight white blazer that narrows at her thin waist before flaring out at her hips. A black shirt with a cowl neck is under the blazer.

"Morgan?"

Her eyes widen in surprise. "Brandon? What on earth are you doing here? I thought you were still in Star Lake."

She really has been out of touch. "I moved to Dallas after you left. I've been working for an ad firm there, but I just got hired by Bling Inc., and they moved us up here."

If my barb about her leaving us affected her, she doesn't show it. "That's wonderful, Brandon. I always knew you could do great things if you put your mind to it."

Her words bother me, though I'm not exactly sure why. More pressing on my mind is why she's here. "Thanks, Morgan, but what are you doing here?"

"Oh, right," she flicks her hand. "I live across the way, and I wondered if I could borrow some creamer for my coffee. I forgot to pick some up on my way home yesterday. You know how I like my coffee with a little bit of sweet."

I narrow my eyes at her. Why is she being so friendly? "I know how you used to like your coffee, but that was four years ago before you up and left Joy and me. I don't know anything about you now."

Her perfectly manicured hand touches my arm. The red on her nails matches the color on her lips. "Don't be like that, Brandon. We're going to be neighbors, at least for a while; we might as well be neighborly." She tries to poke her head around me. "Speaking of Joy, where is she?"

I pull the door closer to me, blocking the view of Joy behind me. "She's here, but I'm not sure I want you seeing her. You put her through hell when you left the first time. I don't want to put her through that again."

A cold gleam flickers in her eye for a moment, and then it's gone. Her hand leaves my arm to flick a dark strand behind her ear. "She's my daughter, Brandon. You can't keep her from me forever."

Icy fear trickles through my body, stirring a cold anger. She better not be trying to take Joy. "You didn't want to be a mother when you left."

Her weight shifts from one foot to the other. "I know, but I was wrong. I've had a lot of time to think about it."

I pull the door completely closed behind me and cross my arms. "You never even bothered to contact us. Not for birthdays or holidays."

Her full lips push out into a pout. "I'm not trying to take her, Brandon. I just thought since we're living right across from each that maybe I could get to know my daughter."

"We'll see," I say. "For now, wait here, and I'll get your creamer."

Without letting her in, I open the door behind me and slip inside, closing it after.

"Who is it, Daddy?" Joy asks. Thankfully, she is still working on her cereal, or she'd have probably run to the door to check the visitor out. I haven't spoken of Morgan since she left, and I have no idea if Joy would remember her or not, but I'm unwilling to chance it right now.

"Just a neighbor looking to borrow some creamer." I open the large black fridge and scan the door. There's a bottle of Peppermint creamer situated snugly between some strawberry jelly and a bottle of ketchup. Plucking it from the shelf, I close the fridge and cross back to the front door.

Morgan still waits on the other side. I shove the creamer into her hands, anxious to be rid of her for now, until I can sort out my feelings. "I have to get back to her, but we'll talk later." Without waiting to hear an excuse from her, I step back in the apartment and close the door.

I lean against the closed door and run my hand over my face. Morgan. Back in my life. I was not expecting this, and I have no idea how I feel about it.

The clatter of the bowl falling into the sink breaks my thoughts. Joy is smiling sheepishly at me from the sink. "Sorry, Daddy."

"It's okay, bug. How about we get dressed and see what there is to do around here, huh?"

"Okay." She shrugs, and her voice is flatter than normal.

I had been hoping for more enthusiasm, but I'm sure the city will grow on her.

After we are both dressed, I peek out the hole in the door. Morgan is no longer standing in the hallway, but I wonder if she'll be watching for us to leave. I open the door slowly and scan the hallway before pulling Joy out the door and locking it behind us.

As my finger presses the elevator button, I worry that Morgan will be in the car when it opens, but when the door slides open, there is no one inside. My heart resumes its normal beating.

Five minutes later, we are exiting the lobby into the cold New York air. Dirty snow lines the sidewalks from a previous storm, creating a cloudy white atmosphere. We join the steady stream of people heading right. Joy clasps my hands tightly as people push past us. Smells from the neighboring restaurants compete against each other as we pass their doors.

After a few blocks, Joy begins slowing down. I slow my pace to match hers, sure there is a park nearby. It finally appears after another block, a small play structure surrounded by patches of white left-over snow.

A gaggle of women I assume are nannies surround one bench. One or two push strollers back and forth with one hand. A few children Joy's age and younger play on the playground, in careful view of the nannies.

"Can I play for a little bit, Daddy?" Joy's energy has suddenly returned as she bounces up and down and tugs on my hand.

"Of course, bug, that's why we're here."

She drops my hand and takes off like a rocket. Within minutes, she has found a friend on the playground and is running around playing hide and seek with the girl. I wander to the other unoccupied park bench and take a seat.

While I watch Joy play, I slip my phone out, hoping to see a message from Presley, but there is nothing. I know I was awful the day she came to say she wasn't coming, but I had hoped that she would change her mind and at least come see if she liked New York, but she is stubborn. Probably as stubborn as I am. Before I can stop them, my fingers fly across the keyboard with a mind of their own. "I wanted to say I'm sorry, and I miss you. We made it. We're staying at the Stratton apartments if you change your mind. Thirtieth floor, number two. I know Joy would love to see you, as would I." They pause for a moment and then hit the send button. My eyes are glued to the phone waiting for the little white circle with a check mark to turn blue. It does, and I wait another minute, but no reply comes.

The phone is almost back in my pocket when it rings. "Hello?" I hadn't dared look at the caller ID. Could I be so lucky as to think about Presley and make her call?

"Brandon? It's Stewart." My heart falls. "I need you to come in tomorrow for a few hours to get familiarized and get the paperwork in order."

I glance over at Joy. "I don't have a nanny yet, Stewart. Can it wait a few days?"

"I'm sorry. It can't. Isn't there someone who could watch her for a few hours?"

My mind flicks to Morgan. Could I trust her for a few hours with Joy? She is her mother, and she had seemed interested in getting to know her, but what if she tells Joy? It took a long time to get Joy to stop asking about her mother, and I don't know what it would do to a five-year old psyche to come face to face with the woman who left you. "Maybe. Let me check, and I'll call you back later."

I punch the end button and tuck the phone back in my pocket. My hands follow; the air here is colder than I expected, and I hadn't dressed for warmth. Joy hadn't either, and a few minutes later she returns, cheeks and nose red with cold.

"Daddy, can we go home? I'm cold."

"Of course, bug."

That night, after laying Joy down, I venture across the hall and knock on the other door. Morgan swings the door open, a smile lighting her face as she sees me. She has changed out of her white suit into a pair of pink sweats that hug her slim hips and a cropped tee. Her stomach shows no signs of ever birthing a child. I pull my eyes from her toned abs to find a bemused look on her face.

"What can I do for you, Brandon?"

"Were you serious earlier when you said you wanted to get to know Joy?"

"Absolutely."

I take a deep breath. Every fiber in my body screams this is a bad idea, but I see no other choice. "I have to go into work for a few hours tomorrow, and I haven't found a nanny for Joy yet. Would you be available to watch her?"

Her mouth opens, but before she can answer, I hold up my hand. "There are a few things you'd have to promise me. You can't tell her who you are yet. I will tell her, but I need to figure out the best way, and you have to stay in the apartment."

"I can do that. What time do you need me?"

I had set the meeting time for during Joy's nap. She didn't nap long anymore, but she almost always laid down for thirty to forty-five minutes right after lunch. "Twelve-thirty pm. I should only be a few hours, and she should nap at least a little of that."

"Don't worry." Her hand finds my arm again. "I have been around kids before. It will be fine."

Her words do nothing to soften the unease developing in my stomach, but I nod, extricate her hand, and thank her. As I walk back to my apartment, I feel as if I've just made a deal with the devil.

Chapter Twenty-Two - Presley

My stomach is a bundle of nerves as I take my seat on the airplane. I gave Trudy a crash course in how to run the shop while I'm gone, and though I know nothing terrible will happen, I can't help feeling as if I've forgotten to tell her something important. I run through the list in my head. I gave her a copy of the key; I told her about wrapping up the pastries each night; and I even left her a few recipes in case she must make more, though I doubt I'll be gone that long. I showed her where the price list was and how to use the register.

"Where are you headed, dearie?" The woman beside me is older with white hair and a kind face.

"New York." I slide my bag under the seat and buckle my belt. "How about you?"

"The same. My granddaughter is graduating from design school."

"Oh, that's wonderful. Congratulations." My fingers tap on my leg, and I reach down to pull a book from my bag. I rarely have time to read anymore, but long flights are always good for that.

"You seem nervous." The older woman smiles. "You must be going to see a man."

My head swivels to her, my eyes wide. "How could you possibly know that?"

She laughs; the sound is a pleasant throaty chuckle. "I raised four girls. I can always tell when it's a man. Do you love him?"

A heat flares across my cheeks. "I do, at least I think I do. I love him when he's himself, but he took this job, and this side of him – I'm not so sure." My hands clench the book, folding it into a cylindrical shape.

The woman nods as if she understands my incoherent babble. Maybe she does after raising four girls.

"And you're going to find out?"

"I am. He asked me to come and gave me his apartment name, but I didn't tell him I was coming. I wanted to surprise him and Joy, that's his daughter." I have no idea why I am sharing all of this with a complete stranger, but my mouth seems incapable of shutting.

"Ah, there's a child involved," the woman says, her eyebrow arching. "That makes it even harder." The way she looks at me makes me wonder if she has experience in this area too.

As the plane takes off, I find myself sharing the whole story with her. She listens, nodding at all the right places, and interjecting her opinion when I pause. Then she tells me about her daughters, and before I know it, the plane is landing. My book remains closed on my lap. *Oh well, another time.*

"I'll be thinking about you tomorrow," she says as we gather our bags. "I hope everything works out for you."

"Me too."

As I navigate through the crowded airport, my heart begins to pull tighter. I wonder if I should call him and let him know I'm in town. I don't know what his work schedule is; he didn't say in the text, but I'm afraid he will say he can't see me. I've already come all this way.

After grabbing my suitcase from the baggage claim, I weave through the throng of people over to the transportation desk. A frazzled woman with a pair of black glasses that keep sliding down her petite nose is behind the giant desk.

As I stand in the line, my eyes scan the surroundings. A board advertising local hotels with a phone in the center catches my eye. Stepping out of the line, I move closer and realize I can use this phone to call for a van to my hotel. I'm glad I thought to book one ahead of time.

I pick up the phone and dial *63 for the Marriott Hotel. It was the closest one to Brandon's apartment building, and since I am unfamiliar with New York, I didn't want to tempt getting lost on my way there.

"Marriott Hotel, how may I help you?"

"Hello, my name is Presley Hays. I have a reservation for tonight. I just arrived at the airport and was hoping a shuttle could come and get me."

"Of course, what kiosk are you at?"

Kiosk? I scan the area for a number. "Um, I'm not sure. I'm calling from the phone by baggage claim three."

"Is there a number and letter combination on the phone you're holding?" The woman's voice is patient. She must deal with people like me all the time.

I hold the phone out and there is indeed a white strip on the back with G7 typed in black letters. "G7. I'm at G7."

"Wonderful. I'll tell the shuttle driver. It's a black van with the Marriott logo on the side. Please go out and wait by the post with G7 on it. He should be there momentarily."

"Thank you." I replace the phone and grab the handle of my wheeled suitcase.

The air is cold as I exit the airport. I pull my coat tighter and wish I'd put on my gloves and hat before exiting the building. Concrete posts line the area, and I make my way to the one with G7 in big blue letters. Four lanes of traffic lay in front of me, and my mind boggles at the sheer number of cars jockeying for position. If traffic is bad here, I'm not sure I want to see how it is on the city streets.

A few minutes later, the black van pulls up, and I flash a small wave at the driver. He puts the van in park and comes around to open the door and help with my luggage. He is a squat man with thinning brown hair. His white top stretches across his belly, the buttons nearly bursting at the seams. A black vest with the Marriott logo covers some of his shirt but has no chance of meeting in the middle.

I climb into the van and squeeze down between two other passengers. "Hi, thank you," I say, but receive only grunts in response. New York is certainly different from Star Lake.

The traffic is just as bad as I imagined, and it takes over half an hour to get to our destination. While the people beside me are glued to their smart phones, my eyes are focused on the world outside. There are so many lights and even this late in the evening, a sea of people swarms the sidewalks. How can Brandon want to live here?

When the van parks in front of the hotel, I wait for the other people to disembark before grabbing my bag and stepping down. "Thank you very much," I say to the driver, placing a tip in his hand.

His other hand covers mine. "Don't lose yourself here." The seriousness in his brown eyes chills my soul, but I nod. He releases my hand, hands me my luggage, and climbs back in the driver's seat leaving me standing on the sidewalk as the people part around me, either ignoring me entirely or shooting glares my direction.

When the tide slows, I skirt into the hotel door, which is opened by a tall thin man in a smart burgundy uniform. "Welcome to the Marriott, miss."

"Thank you." The lobby unfolds before me, and my eyes widen. Two white candelabras hang from the ceiling. A fountain issuing crystal blue water takes up one corner. A white couch and a few lounging chairs sit around a glass coffee table under one chandelier.

Towards the back, a row of computers lines a table. On the right, a gleaming gold and white desk fills most of the real estate. A man and a woman stand behind it, serving the customers in the line.

I join the queue, my eyes still large as I take in the rest of the opulent surroundings.

"Can I help you?"

Startled, I turn to the woman behind the counter. Her auburn hair is pulled back in a tight bun and her skin is flawless except for a dusting of freckles across her nose. The tiny typed tag on her fitted jacket reads Kaya.

"Hi, yes, I'm Presley Hays, and I have a reservation for tonight."

She nods and begins tapping away on her keyboard. "Will you be staying with us just one night, Ms. Hays?"

I hesitate. I have no idea how long I'll be staying. My hope is it will be more than one night, but what if Brandon has changed his mind or what if I hate it here and change my mind. "I'm not sure."

She smiles at my indecision. "That's fine. We're not booked right now, so if you decide to stay longer, it should be no problem."

"Thank you."

She nods and finishes checking me in before printing off a contract sheet, which I sign and hand back to her. After processing my payment, she hands me the key card and points the way to the elevator.

My shoes echo on the marble flooring as I make my way to the elevator. I punch the round button to go up, and a moment later, the bell dings. The cab inside is lavish with dark carpet and a white and gold wallpaper on the walls. Stepping in, I punch the button for twenty-one, and the door closes.

When it opens again, I'm on the twenty-first floor where the dark carpet continues into the hallway. A gold-plated sign points me to the right for room 2103.

After inserting the key, I push open the door to a large hotel room. The queen bed doesn't even fill half of the room. A large mahogany dresser sits across from it and above the dresser is a big screen TV. Next to the bed is a matching dresser that holds an ornate lamp, and against the window is a matching table.

To my right, a door opens to a large bathroom and to the left is a large closet. Wheeling the suitcase in, I heft it into the chair at the table and pull out my sleepwear and my toothbrush. I've never been able to sleep at night without brushing my teeth. The one time I tried, the fuzzy feeling on my teeth kept me awake all night long.

It is still early, but I haven't slept well the last few nights, and I want to make sure I'm up early to do some shopping for Brandon and Joy.

The sheets on the bed are like heaven, and my eyes close as soon as my head hits the pillow.

The blaring alarm clock wakes me the next morning, Yawning, I stretch my stiff back and sore shoulders. The cramped seats of airplanes always wreak havoc on me the next day.

I pad into the bathroom and turn the shower on. The warm water erases the last remnant of sleep from my eyes, and when it is over, I feel refreshed and ready, though still nervous.

After a quick breakfast, I push open the doors and join the crowd on the sidewalk. The chilly wind nips at my face, and I slink further down in my coat, wishing I had brought a scarf. Perhaps I'll add that to my list.

I have a map in my pocket of how to get to Brandon's apartment building that I printed at one of the computers in the hotel lobby before embarking, but I want to stop and get their Christmas gifts as well. The computer had said there were a few shops along the route, and I am hopeful they will have what I'm looking for.

The toy shop appears on my right first, and with a quick maneuver, I duck inside. A gust of warm heater air hits me as the doors close behind me, and I unzip my coat. Rows and rows of shelves line the store with colorful toys and games. I scan the aisle headings that hang on square signs suspended from the ceiling.

As I enter the correct aisle, my eyes widen at the sheer number of puzzles. They line the shelves on either side from floor to about eight feet. A myriad of colors and picture options stare back at me, but I know exactly what I would love to find. Slowly, I saunter down the aisle, head swiveling from left to right and top to bottom until my eyes alight on it. It's perfect, and though it's a thousand pieces – bigger than any she has done so far – I just know that Joy will love it.

I grasp it like a cherished doll as I return to the front check out and join the long line. Evidently, other people had the same idea I did. Reaching the front of the queue, I pass the box to the young red-headed man who is running the register.

"Is there any chance I can get it gift wrapped?" I ask.

He flicks agitated green eyes up at me and sighs. "Yes, I'll add in the charge, and you can take it to Patrice near the back. She's wrapping."

"Thank you." I hand over my credit card, and after signing, I take the box the direction he has pointed. The line here is shorter, and I'm in front of Patrice within five minutes.

"Hi," she says smiling up at me. "Do you have a paper preference?" Her smile is warm, but her brown eyes look tired.

"It's for a girl," I say handing over the box.

Nodding, she turns in her chair and grabs a roll of silver paper with pink trees. She holds it up for my approval, and I nod. "Fill out a tag, and pick a bow," she says, pointing to a bin of both beside her at the table.

After selecting a pink bow, I grab a white tag with snowflakes on it and fill out "To Joy, From Presley."

Minutes later, I am walking back out into the frigid air, my newly wrapped package beneath my arm. Brandon's gift will be a little harder, but I'm hopeful a store with a Christmas section will have what I'm looking for.

Another block up on the right, I see a Christmas outlet store. Surely, they will have something similar to the picture in my mind.

The store is large and full of everything Christmas you could wish for. There are trees, ornaments, stockings, lights, hats, and more. I find myself wandering up and down the aisles looking at all the intricate ornaments. Christmas has long been my favorite time of year.

Near the end of the third aisle, I see it. A glass ornament with a boy and girl kissing inside as snow falls on them. It reminds me of our first kiss in Star Lake, and it's perfect. The couple even reminds me a little of us.

I take the ornament to the counter and repeat the process of paying for it and getting it wrapped. The lady is nice enough to hand me a tote bag to carry both Brandon's and Joy's present.

My stomach rumbles as I hit the sidewalk again, letting me know that too much time has passed, and lunch is now in order.

I stop at a bistro just down the street from Brandon's apartment building, and as I eat my turkey and ham on sourdough, I gather my courage to finish the journey. My heart tells me he'll be happy to see me, but my head is saying I should have responded to his text.

I swallow the last bite of sandwich down with a helpful swig of my iced tea and then gather my trash and my bag. A few minutes later, I stand in front of Brandon's apartment building.

A man in a maroon suit, like the one at the hotel I'm staying at opens the door for me. The inside is as impressive as the lobby of my hotel, but I have no time to admire the view. My heart is pounding in my chest as I bypass the front desk and follow the signs to the elevator. I have no idea if I'm supposed to check in, but I hope that if I just look like I belong that no one will stop me.

As the elevator door opens, I turn right down the hallway. With each step toward the white door, the pounding in my head grows louder. Sweat breaks out on my hands, and a solitary bead rolls down my spine.

My hand raps the door three times, and I wait. When it swings open, the bag nearly tumbles from my hand.

"Morgan?" The words come out as a tortured whisper. I can't believe my eyes, and I fight the urge to rub them and hope the nightmare disappears.

"Why, hello Presley." Her voice sounds sweet but her blue eyes are cold as ice. Her perfect figure is accentuated in her tight t-shirt and pants. Her dark hair is perfectly curled and lays seductively across her shoulder.

"What are you doing here, Morgan?" The words are a little more forceful this time, but my entire body is shaking with the strain of not punching Morgan's perfect nose.

"I could ask you the same thing." Her voice is smug, and she leans against the door as if the apartment is hers.

"I'm here to see Brandon and Joy." Anger is boiling up inside me, threatening to spill over any moment.

Her eyes widen in false regret. "Oh, now's not a good time. We are having some family time. You see, now that we're back in the same city, we've decided to reunite our family."

Her words knock the air out of me, and my hand reaches for the wall to steady my weak knees. Why wouldn't Brandon have told me? Why would he ask me to come? The logical part of my brain insists that something isn't right, but the emotional side sees Morgan in his apartment. Why else would she be here? The need to vomit burns in my throat.

I hold out the bag, unable to remain any longer in the hallway. "Tell him I said hi then and give him these, will you?"

"Of course." Her smile is like a predator's before it devours its prey.

Numb, I turn and walk back down the hallway, barely registering the click of the closing door behind me. My hand presses the elevator button with no conscious thought from me, and the walk back to my hotel is a blur.

Why would he be back together with Morgan? Had I meant so little to him? It doesn't matter. I shouldn't have come, and this must be the sign that I should have stayed back in Star Lake and moved on.

When the door to my hotel room opens, I enter, letting the force of the door close it behind me and throw myself on the bed. I know I'll need to schedule my tickets for tomorrow, but first I need another good cry. I curl into a ball and let the tears flow silently down my cheeks.

Chapter Twenty-Three

~ Brandon

"How was your day, bug?" I ask Joy after Morgan has gone.

"It was okay." Her words are nonchalant, but the accompanying shrug tells me it wasn't the best day.

"Did you not like Morgan?"

"She was alright, but not like Presley. She didn't play with me or talk to me like Presley does."

With a sigh, I sink down on the couch, which looks much more comfortable than it is, and take Joy in my arms. "I know, honey. I thought Presley would at least come and see us, but I think I messed it up too badly."

Joy leans her head against my shoulder. "Me too. I should have told her I wanted her to be my mom."

Her words prick like a thorn in my heart. *If this job is so good, then why are we both so sad?*

After putting Joy to bed, I return to the couch and flick on the television. I've just gotten comfortable when a knock sounds at the door. Tossing the remote on the couch beside me, I cross to the door and peek out the spyhole.

I sigh as I see Morgan on the other side. "What can I do for you, Morgan?" I ask as I open the door.

She smiles and holds out a basket full of muffins. "I wanted to say thank you for letting me watch Joy this afternoon. I thought maybe we could talk?" Her attire is more casual today, just an oversized t-shirt over a pair of leggings. Perhaps she has changed, at least a little.

I step back and hold the door open. Hearing her out surely won't hurt anything. Joy is asleep, and it's not like I had anything else to do. She closes the door behind her and follows me to the living room, where I resume my position on the couch. After taking the other end, she hands out the basket, and I select a muffin. I unwrap it and take a bit. While good, it is not the same as Presley's homemade muffins, and it just makes me miss her more.

"So, I wanted to apologize again for leaving four years ago," Morgan says as she unwraps her own muffin. "I was selfish, and I shouldn't have done that to you or to Joy." She plucks off a tiny morsel from her muffin and puts it in her mouth.

I want to tell her 'no kidding,' but she does appear to be trying, so I swallow the spiteful words and try again. "It was hard, Morgan. Harder than you'll probably ever know. Joy cried for months after you left, but finally she got over it and seems to have either forgotten or moved on. That's why I don't want you saying anything yet. It needs to be done right."

"Of course, you're right," she says, folding the rest of her muffin back up in the wrapper and setting it beside her. "I wouldn't want to do anything to damage her further. Is there any way I can make it up to her? Or to you?" She shifts closer to me as she says these words, and her hand touches my knee.

"Morgan, don't."

"Don't what?" She bats her eyes at me, pretending not to know what I'm talking about.

I shoot her a pointed stare and then look down at her hand. "You know what."

"Don't you think we owe it to ourselves to see if we could be a family again? I mean, I've changed, and you're successful now."

Her words strike a chord in me, and I push her hand away. "And what if I lose this job? Would you walk out on us again?" The irritation is quickly shifting to full-blown anger.

"You wouldn't."

"You can't know that Morgan." My voice comes out as a hiss as I try to keep the volume down so as not to wake Joy. "You can't control what might happen, and I can't take the chance of you deciding our life doesn't suit yours anymore and leaving again, but since it is what you seem to do best, I think it's time you leave now." I stand and wait for her to follow suit.

Her mouth opens as if she has more to say, though what she could possibly say now is beyond me. With a sigh, she shuts her mouth and stands up. "I'm sorry. I'm saying everything wrong, but I'll keep working Brandon. I want us to be a family again." She touches my arm again on her way out, and it takes all my reserve not to shake her hand off.

After closing the door behind her, I pull out my phone and stare at it. I miss Presley more than ever now, and more than just her, I miss being able to tell her whatever is on my mind. Morgan reappearing has affected me, and I just wish I could discuss it with Presley. She would know what to do.

Though I didn't end it well, Presley never said I couldn't call her. My teeth rake across my bottom lip as I enter the bedroom and sit on the big bed. A swipe of the screen shows no new calls or messages, but I desperately miss my friend. I'd forgotten how much until she walked back into my life.

Swallowing my pride, I dial the number, hoping she'll pick up. My heart drops as her voice mail kicks on. *Do I leave a message? I can't say anything about Morgan on a message, but maybe she'll call me back.* "Hey, Presley, it's me, Brandon. I left you a text, but never heard back from you. We miss you. Joy and me. We'd love to see you if you get a chance. Okay, well you know where we are."

I punch the end call button feeling like an idiot and wishing there was a way to delete the idiotic message, but I know it's already gone through the airwaves.

The next morning, the nanny search begins. Stewart gave me until the day after Christmas to get one hired, and then I must return to work. Leaving Joy with anyone makes me uneasy. It took me ages to find Amber, and I can't imagine how long it will take here in New York where people are much more uptight and hard to read.

The first knock comes at eight am. A nice-looking woman in a tie-dyed shirt is on the other side. "I'm Amelia, and I'm totally stoked to meet you."

As she sticks out her hand, the smell of weed carries over. No way am I leaving my daughter with someone who shows up to an interview stoned.

"Sorry, we're no longer looking." I shut the door before she has a chance to respond and shake my head. Marijuana isn't even legal in New York, but ever since Washington and Colorado made it legal, people have been bolder everywhere.

"You didn't like that one?" Joy asks, looking up from her cereal.

"Not even a little." I ruffle her hair and grab my coffee mug for a quick sip before the next knock.

This time the woman is severe looking with her hair pulled back in a tight bun and angry lines filling her face.

"I don't do laundry or cook or change diapers," she says as she shoves her resume at me.

"Good thing Joy is five then." She doesn't catch my humor and appraises Joy over my shoulder. The disapproving stare she gives my daughter is enough to end the interview. "We'll be in touch."

"What was wrong with that one?" Joy has finished her cereal and is washing her bowl in the sink. I'm taken aback by how grown up she seems sometimes.

"I didn't like the look she gave you, like she wanted to change you. You are perfect just the way you are."

She rolls her eyes. "Da-ad." The word is drawn out to two syllables the way she says it.

"I'm sorry. I'm going to be picky because you are the most important thing to me."

"That's not true." Her words surprise me. "If I was, we would have stayed in Star Lake with Presley."

"Joy – " I'm interrupted by another knock at the door. Sighing, I hold my finger up to tell her the discussion is not done and cross to the front door. A blond woman with the surprised expression of too many Botox injections is on the other side, dressed impeccably in some ridiculous designer jumpsuit.

"Hi, I'm Alex. I'm here about the nanny job." She extends a slender hand with a French manicure.

She is too perfect for my choice, but I have yet to interview anyone. I might as well give her a whirl. "Brandon." I clasp her hand and shake. Her face grimaces from my grip. "Come in." Holding the door open, I step back.

Her kitten heels click on the floor as she enters the apartment. Her eyes scan the room appreciatively. "Nice place."

"It's only on loan for a few weeks until our stuff arrives and we get settled."

"I see, and where will you be locating to?" Her voice holds just the smallest hint of disgust that this isn't our permanent home.

"I'm not sure. I guess I should start looking."

Her slender eyebrow raises at me. "If you want a good place, you should."

I don't like the way she is appearing to judge me, but after glancing at her resume, she seems solid. The Botox makes her look younger than her experience shows. She has evidently nannied for some high-profile people in the city, at least if her resume is truthful.

"Right, well why don't you tell me what a day would look like in your book?"

She folds her hands together. "I believe in schedules, so your child would eat breakfast at eight am. Then we would spend an hour reading or doing school work. I believe exercise is important, so then we would walk to the nearest park for an hour. Lunch would be after that, and then the child would nap. If you allow television, they would get an hour after lunch. Then there is free play time and crafts."

My mind is dizzy trying to keep up with her schedule, but there could be worse things.

"My resume has references you can call. I'm very dedicated."

"Why did you leave your last job?" Everything on paper seemed right, but if she were so perfect, why was she free?

"My last family just moved. As you can see, I was with them for three years." She points to the bottom of the resume, the last job entry.

"Well, Alex, everything looks good. I'd like to contact your references, and of course, I'm sure there will still be more interviews today. Can I call you tomorrow?"

"Of course. I'll be at my mother's house in Brooklyn for Christmas Eve and Christmas, but I'm not leaving until late on the twenty-third."

The twenty-third? Is it that close to Christmas already? I haven't decorated the apartment at all for Christmas. I shake hands with Alex and walk her to the door, making an impromptu decision that she will do. I want to take Joy out to get a tree and some decorations; I can't let her first Christmas in New York be un-Christmassy.

When the door closes behind Alex, I dial the agency I had called for nannies and ask them not to send any more prospects out. "Joy, bundle up. We're going to get a tree."

Joy looks up from the dolls she had been playing with on the living room floor. "We're getting a tree?"

"Yes, hopefully we can find a lot that still has one. Hurry up."

"A lot? You mean we can't cut one down like we did at Nana's." Her face scrunches in confusion.

"Sorry, bug, there are no forests around here, but we'll find a good one at a lot."

She looks unsure, but runs to her room to get her coat and hat. I grab mine off the rack, and by the time I have it on, she has returned. I close and lock the door behind us.

"Well, hello there."

I freeze at the sound of Morgan's voice. I was hoping not to run into her; I'm still frustrated by her insinuation last night, and I don't want Joy finding out who she is yet. I'm also still not certain she isn't trying to take Joy away.

"Hi, Morgan." I keep my eyes on the floor in hopes she will get the hint, but she doesn't. As she sidles up to me at the elevator, I can smell her perfume. Something strong and heavy. My eyes flick her direction long enough to take in her tight shirt with a low cowl neck and her skin tight white pants. She is still beautiful, but it no longer affects me. She seems too done up. I miss Presley's easy going way. She could be ready in ten minutes for whatever we wanted to do, and she'd never be caught dead in skin tight white pants.

"Where are you guys headed?" She takes another step closer, so that her arm is touching mine.

"We're going to get a tree," Joy pipes up. I had been hoping she would keep that information to herself.

The elevator dings, and we step inside. I punch the button for the lobby.

"What a coincidence," Morgan says, "I was just going out to find a tree too. I know of a wonderful lot. They have the best trees. Maybe we can go together." Her hand finds my arm, and she bats her eyes up at me.

I don't want to say yes, but it would be incredibly rude to say no now, and I have no idea where to go. "Sure, Morgan, that sounds nice."

She squeezes my arm, but instead of a lover's touch, it feels like claws digging into my skin. I have a hard time believing I fell in love with this woman six years ago, but I can't hate her too much because she did give me Joy.

When the doors open again, Morgan leads the way out of the elevator cab. The swiveling of her hips is meant for me, and while I can appreciate the view, it does nothing for me.

"Mark," she calls, "be a dear and fetch me my coat."

Mark tips his hat and exits the room, returning a moment later with a long blue Burberry hooded trench coat. A ring of fur surrounds the inside of the hood. He holds it out for her, and she slips her arms in.

As I watch the display, a bubble of nausea develops in my stomach. Was she always this spoiled? I try to think back to when we first met, but the memories are hazy.

"Shall we?"

Nodding, I hold out my hand for her to lead the way. Joy clutches my other tightly as if it's a life line. We follow Morgan and Mark out of the hotel. I wonder why he's still with us until I see him hailing a cab for us. *Of course, heaven forbid she hail her own cab.* After Morgan climbs in, I send Joy in before climbing in myself. My hope is that Joy's presence will be a buffer and keep Morgan's hands off me.

Joy's eyes are wide as we buckle up, and they grow wider still as the cab weaves in and out of traffic. A few minutes later, we stop in front of a tree lot situated snugly between two buildings. The lot is half empty, but the selection that is left appears worthy.

Morgan pays the cabbie, and we climb out of the car. Joy pulls on my hand, excited to see the trees. Laughing, I allow her to lead me to the lot. She peruses each tree carefully as if judging them in a contest.

"They aren't as nice as the ones in the woods, are they?"

Though serious, her question makes me laugh. "No, I guess not quite."

She nods like she expected that answer and continues her critiquing.

"I didn't get a chance to ask you last night, but how have you been?" Morgan asks. Joy has dropped my hand, but I make sure to keep her close in my sight.

"You mean since you left?" My voice is barely above a whisper as I don't want Joy to hear.

Morgan rolls her eyes. "Sure, if you want to go back that far."

"Well, let's see. After you left, I couldn't bear to stay in Star Lake, so I packed up my one-year-old daughter and moved to Dallas. I got a job at a promotions firm and had to hire a nanny to watch her while I worked all day, something I always thought her mother would do. My father fell off a ladder, and I had to return to Star Lake. I ran into Presley Hays, remember her?" Morgan's face pinches into a tight smile, and she nods. There was no love lost between those two, though I never understood why until now. "Then I returned to Dallas to do the presentation for Stewart, and he offered me the job here, and here we are."

"Are you ever going to forgive me for leaving?" Morgan asks. "I really am trying to be better." Her claws have once again found my arm, and I shake them off.

"I'm sure you are, Morgan, but I need someone stable for Joy, someone I know will be there for the long haul."

Her lips form a tight smile. "I've changed, Brandon. You should really consider giving me a chance."

Thankfully, I am saved from answering by Joy's call. "I think this is the best one, Daddy." Relieved, I catch up to her and appraise the tree myself. It's not as nice as the one we cut down in the woods, but it's decent for a lot tree.

"Okay, this one it is." I grab the tag, blinking at the price tag of one hundred dollars. Things are certainly expensive here in New York. Hoisting the tree, I take it to the checkout table. After charging my card, the man twines it up, and I throw it back over my shoulder. Morgan plucks a tag off a tree, not even bothering to check it out and hands it to the man who gets the tree and wraps it up for her. Then he passes the tree to an associate who carries it out for Morgan as we stroll back to the sidewalk to hail a cab home.

The tree man helps secure the trees on the roof of the cab, and Morgan slips him a bill for his trouble. Then she whips out her phone and taps off a text. As we pull up to the apartments, I realize she has texted Mark as he stands waiting for us. He takes Morgan's tree as I grab mine and the stand I purchased from the lot. I shake my head at Morgan's inability to do anything for herself as I lead the way to the elevator.

We part ways at the thirtieth floor – Mark taking Morgan's tree to the left, and I taking our tree to the right. Joy and I set the tree up, and when it is secure, we begin cutting off the twine. With a few snips, the tree expands, sending a shower of pine needles across the floor.

"Well, what do you think?" I ask her.

She stares at the tree, her finger tapping her chin. "It needs ornaments."

I agree, but I don't dare chance another meeting with Morgan. "We'll go tomorrow."

Chapter Twenty-Four - Presley

"Oh, no, what happened?" Trudy's face is a canvas of empathy.

Mine is probably still red and splotchy from all the tears it has shed the last few days. I shake my head at her. "I'm so stupid. I flew all the way across the country, but he had already moved on."

"What are you talking about? He may be an idiot for taking that job, but the man was clearly in love with you." She wraps her arm about my shoulders as we walk to the baggage claim to grab my suitcase.

"Morgan answered the door."

"Morgan?"

"Yeah, Joy's mother. She said they found each other and now they're working on reuniting as a family."

"Well, I don't know about you, but she didn't seem exactly trustworthy from what I remember." Trudy drops her arm from my shoulder to punch the elevator button.

"It doesn't matter," I shrug as we step inside the silver box. "Even if she was lying, I lost him once to her. Why would I stand a chance living over fifteen hundred miles away while she is right in the city with her perfect hair and her perfect figure?"

"Stop being so hard on yourself. You're beautiful too."

She's trying to cheer me up, so I try not to roll my eyes too hard. "He made his choice. I'll just have to deal with it and move on." The elevator door opens, and we continue down the hallway to the baggage claim area. It is nearly devoid of people, but a few stand waiting at the one silver carousel.

The baggage carousel starts up, cutting off any further conversation. We watch in silence as the bags tumble down the black ramp onto the circling silver track. When mine appears, I step forward and haul it from the carousel. "Okay," I sigh. "Let's go home."

The hour ride from the airport is quiet. I spend most of the time staring at the lack of scenery out the window, and I'm sure Trudy is spending it trying to come up with words to mend my thrice broken heart.

She gives me a hug at the driveway, and I head into my apartment alone. When the door closes behind me, I pull my phone from my pocket and play Brandon's message again. He called last night when I was pigging out on ice cream in my hotel room. I hadn't had the courage to take the call, in case he was calling to tell me himself about Morgan, but I had listened to it after. Again and again. His voice had sounded sincere, but he'd said nothing about Morgan. Could it be then that Morgan had lied? That they weren't together. If so, though, why was she in his apartment?

Frustrated and confused, I punch the end button on my phone and haul my luggage into my room. After hoisting it on the bed, I begin unpacking it. The clothes barely had time to get wrinkled as I had just put them in the suitcase two days ago. I shake my head, still unable to believe I hopped on a plane to see a man only to hop on the next one out. What a waste of time and money.

My sleep is restless that night, just as it was last night. I wonder if I'll ever sleep well again. I grab the phone from the nightstand where it is charging and listen to Brandon's voicemail again. My hand hovers over the call back button, but in the end, I decide to replace the phone on the nightstand without calling or texting him. Maybe it's my stubborn pride, but after traveling across the country, I feel that the next move should be his.

I wake before the alarm the next day, and in a daze, I saunter into the bathroom to get dressed for the day. After a cup of coffee, I throw on my coat and begin the walk into town.

"Ah, Presley, you're back. How did it go?" Max is sweeping a light snow off the sidewalk in front of his door. His flannel today is a green and white plaid, but his ball cap is the same blue one he wears every day.

"Not well," I say, forcing a smile on my face. "Maybe I'm just meant to be single."

He motions me inside. The diner is quiet with only the two of us inside. The chairs are still up on the tables. He flips two over and motions for me to sit.

"Look," he says, "I know we aren't the same age, and this whole topic makes me uncomfortable, but I used to feel that way too. I'm sure you know that I pined after Layla for years."

"That's an understatement," I say under my breath.

His face pulls into a glare, wrinkling his forehead. "All I'm saying is, give Brandon time. He'll come around. Love has a way of working things out."

"And if that doesn't work, I'm always available."

Max and I both jump as Bert pops out from a booth.

"Bert, what are you doing there?" Max's face is red with anger or exasperation. It's hard to tell.

"Well, I came in early for the first pot of coffee. The first pot is always the best before it sticks to the bottom and gets metallic tasting, but you weren't here yet, so I curled up in this booth to catch a little more sleep until you arrived."

"How did you get in here? Never mind, I don't want to know." Max rolls his eyes and shakes his head.

"I appreciate the offer, Bert," I say as he turns his eyes on me, "but my heart just got broken again. It's going to need some time to mend, so I think I'm swearing off men for a while."

His brown eyes reminded me of the commercials you see to help fund animal shelters, and I had to fight the urge not to change my mind. Not because I wanted to date him, but because I wanted him to stop making those eyes.

"I should get going; I need to open the bakery. Thanks for the advice Max."

I duck out before either of them can say another word and cross the street to the bakery. Though I've only been gone two days, it feels like a lifetime has passed.

After fumbling with the keys, I manage to open the door and flick the light switch. *Well, Trudy didn't destroy the place. I guess that's good.* The pastry case is empty, so at least she remembered to take them out. Hopefully, she remembered to put them in the fridge.

I drop my bag off in the small office in back and head to the fridge. The pastries are individually wrapped and fill the top shelf. Sighing, I grab them, stacking them in my left arm and head back to the front. One at a time, I peel the saran wrap off and put the pastry back in the case.

The bell jingles as I place the last one. Layla enters, swinging a basket and bearing a smile.

"Oh, good, you're back. Don't get me wrong, I love Trudy, but she had no idea what all the items on my list were. I really missed you." She places the basket on the counter and pulls out a piece of paper – her list.

"At least someone did," I mutter.

"Uh oh, it didn't go well?" Her voice shifts to an empathetic tone.

I shake my head as the tears begin to prick my eyes. There will be no crying at work.

"Well, you know it took Max and I years to find each other. Maybe Brandon will come around, and until then, you have all of us."

The thought brings a small smile to my face, not because I find them fulfilling but because this town is full of quite a cast of characters that pretty much assure there will never be a dull moment.

"Thanks, Layla." I finish packing her bread and pastries in the basket.

"Anytime, kid." With a small wave, she picks the basket back up and exits the building. In true Layla fashion, the room feels darker once she has gone. She has the uncanny ability to light up a room whenever she is in it.

As I wait for the next customer, I pull my phone out of my pocket. A picture of Brandon, Joy, and I with the tree we cut down stares back at me, but there is no message or missed call from Brandon. I should probably change the picture, but I just don't have the heart to take it down. Not yet.

The bell jingles again, and I shove the phone back in my pocket.

"No word yet?" Anna asks. I wasn't quick enough to hide my guilty gesture.

I shake my head. "Nothing since the first night. Do you think I should call him back?"

Anna shrugs. "I honestly don't know anymore. I thought he was going to stay, and you guys would become the couple we all expected. His leaving caught all of us off guard too. Anyway, that's not why I'm here. I know his leaving was hard, but we'd like your family to join us for Christmas. We'd love to have you, and you can bring some chocolate eclairs if you'd like."

Her eyebrows dance as she makes the suggestion, and I can't help but smile. "Deal, although I'm not sure if Mom will be working or not," Unfortunately for my mother, Ryan and I both went to college, so she's still working two jobs to help pay the expenses. I hope one day to be able to repay her some, or at least lighten her load. "but I know Ryan will be free."

She blushes and drops her eyes. "Wonderful. I'll tell Mom, and maybe my brother will come to his senses and come home by then."

As Christmas is only two days away, I highly doubt it, but I don't say anything to Anna. There's no sense spoiling her hope.

The rest of the day is a slow blur, and I'm glad when six hits and I can pack up and go home. Right now, all I want is some chocolate ice cream and Niko on my lap, though I better find another consolation item soon. My pants are already beginning to feel snugger from my ice cream binges the last few days.

Chapter Twenty-Five -
Brandon

"Daddy, when did Presley come by?" Joy asks.

I look up from my phone. "What do you mean, honey? Presley hasn't been here."

"Well, then where did these come from?" She holds out two gifts, a large rectangular box obviously for her with its pink trees and a smaller square box wrapped in green and white striped paper, which I assume is for me.

"Where did you get these?"

"In the closet. I was playing hide and seek with Bunny, and they were there buried under some blankets." She hands me the smaller package. "Can we open them?"

My heart aches at the familiar curve of Presley's letters. It's not Christmas until tomorrow, but I'm curious as to what these are as well. "Yeah, bug, let's see if she left a note with them."

I watch as she tears the paper off the present. Her eyes widen, and a smile lights up her face. "It's perfect." She turns the box to me, and I see the picture of the Eiffel Tower on the puzzle box. A perfect combination of Presley and Joy. The ache grows a little bigger. "Open yours, Daddy."

I pull open the paper to reveal a small white box. Lifting the lid, I peel back the tissue paper and emotion wells inside me. My fingers grasp the tip of the ornament, and I pull it out. The happy couple, so reminiscent of Presley and I stare back at me, and with a flick of my wrist, snow swirls about. It's an image of our first kiss, and it's nearly perfect. My throat constricts with sadness and anger and love. "Where did you say you found these?"

She points behind her. "In the hall closet under some blankets."

Presley had to have come by some time while I was at work and Joy was napping for neither of us to see her, but the only day I've been at work so far was . . . "Morgan." The word comes out more as a threat than a name. "Be right back, bug."

I storm through the door, slamming it behind me, and down the hall to the other end. My knuckles are pounding on the door before I have my words all figured out. It swings open, and Morgan blinks at me.

"Well, hello Brandon, did you change your mind?" She leans seductively against the doorframe, her red lips in a predatory smile.

"When did Presley stop by?"

Her eyes blank for a moment, and her posture shifts. "What do you mean?" Her voice has lost its lusty lilt and now holds an essence of fear.

"I mean we found the presents you hid in the closet. What did you think you were doing?"

She rolls her eyes. "I was protecting you. Presley has always held you back. You're finally doing it right this time; you're in the big leagues. You don't need some small-town girl riding your coattails."

Anger surges through my veins. "What did you tell her?"

Morgan shrugs. "Just that we were working on being a family again."

My hands clench into fists at my side. "Morgan, that's not true. You had no right."

"I had every right. I'm the reason you're even here." Her eyes widen, and her hand flies to her mouth.

"What do you mean you're the reason I'm here?" My voice trails off as Mark's words from the first day come back to me. "You're the owner of the company?" The pieces begin to fall into place. "What did you do, Morgan?"

She takes a deep breath, and her arms fold across her chest. "When I left, it was because I wanted you to see that you could do more. You had gotten used to that sleepy town and you were willing to settle there. I wasn't. I hoped if I left, it would spur you into action, and it did. I followed your move to Dallas and then began working behind the scenes here to get Stewart to meet with you."

"So, my whole career is just because of you." I shake my head at her, not believing she could stoop so low.

"Not your whole career. You still did the work; I just got the connections in front of you."

My hand runs through my hair as I roll my eyes. "It's the same thing, Morgan. I can't believe you thought this would work."

I turn to leave, but her claws reach out and snag my arm. "You can't leave now. If you quit Bling, Inc, your reputation will be ruined."

Slowly, I turn to face her again. "I don't really care, Morgan. My heart isn't here anyway. It's back in Star Lake. With Presley." The truth of my words hit like an anvil over the head. How could I have been so stupid?

After prying her nails off me, I leave Morgan, face gaping in her doorway, and head back to my apartment.

"Joy, how would you feel about getting out of here?"

"Like to the park?" she asks, looking up from her puzzle.

"No," I shake my head, smiling, "I mean home. To Star Lake."

She scrambles up and runs to me, throwing her arms around my legs. "Do you mean it, Daddy?"

I crouch down to wrap my arms around her. "I do, bug. Let's go home."

As she begins packing up her things, I jump on the phone. First to Stewart.

"I'm sorry Stewart, but I can't take the job after all."

"I don't understand. What happened?" His voice is utterly confused on the other end.

"Morgan did, and it's not your fault, but I went down that road once, and I'm not doing it again. Can you give me the name of the moving company, so I can call them to get them to turn around? I'll pay the return trip."

I jot the number down as he rattles it off and thank him before hanging up. The moving company is my next call, and I reach the manager on the second ring.

"I know this is unusual, but I need the drivers to turn around. I need them to go to 812 Cooper Street, Star Lake Texas."

The woman on the other end chuckles. "You'd be surprised. This happens more often than you think. I'll let the driver know right away, but can I ask you one question?"

"Sure." I have no idea what she wants, but the fact that she's so willing to accommodate me makes me more comfortable answering her question.

"Is it for love?"

A smile breaks out on my face, and though I know she can't see it, I'm sure she can hear it in my voice. When I first started sales, that was one of the tricks they taught me. Always smile on the phone because people can hear it in your voice. "Yeah, it is."

"I knew it. It's almost always for love. Good luck."

I thank her and hang up. One more call. After looking up the number on my phone, I dial the airport.

"Customer service, how can I help you?"

"I need to get tickets for the first flight you have to East Texas Regional Airport, and please say it's soon."

"One moment, sir, let me check." I can hear the tapping of keys through the phone. "It looks like there are only two flights a day sir. I can get you on a late flight tonight that leaves at eight pm and would get you into East Texas at eight am. There are two stops, but you won't have to de-plane. Or there is a flight first thing tomorrow at five am that will get you there at four pm. You'd have to change planes once."

I look down at my watch. It's just past noon. There should be plenty of time for us to pack and get to the airport, although there is one more stop I want to make. "I'll take tonight. Two tickets please." I try not to cringe at the price she reads off to me, and I rattle off my credit card. I'll have to find a job quickly in Star Lake, but it will be worth it.

"Okay, you'll need to pick them up at the check in gate, but here's your confirmation number."

After jotting down the number, I end the call and help Joy in her packing. We fill up the suitcases we brought and manage to squeeze in the presents from Presley, but as I look over at the tree, I realize all those presents won't fit.

"We'll have to mail them back, bug. Is that okay?"

"Of course, daddy. None of those hold what I really wanted for Christmas anyway."

"What did you want for Christmas, bug?" I had gotten her the set of books she asked for and a new Barbie.

"I wanted to spend Christmas in Star Lake with Nana and Poppy and Presley."

I scoop her up in a hug and twirl her around the room. "This is going to be the best Christmas ever."

She giggles and squeals as we turn in circles.

"Okay, let me see if I can get a box and have someone take this to the post office. Should we take the ornaments we bought?" We hadn't found many original ones, so they were mainly the colorful balls and a few that looked like icicles.

Her face scrunches, and she shakes her head. "Nah, we can get new ones with Presley."

I sigh. "Bug, we're going back to Star Lake, but I can't guarantee Presley will take me back. You have to be prepared for that."

Joy shakes her head, a knowing smile on her face. She looks so much older than her almost six years. "Daddy, she loves you, and she brought us these presents. She'll take you back."

In my heart, I hope she is right. When I explain what Morgan did, surely Presley will forgive me. "Okay, let me get these presents taken care of then, and we'll head to the airport. We'll have to sleep on the flight, but we'll make it home in time for Christmas."

She smiles and sits on the couch, reading one of her books while I contact Mark and ask him to bring up a box. The knock sounds a moment later. Mark stands on the other side of the door with a large cardboard box in hand.

"Ah, thank you Mark. Can you come in for a minute while I box these up?"

"Of course." He steps inside and closes the door behind him. He stands with his hands behind his back as I back up the few presents under the sparsely decorated tree. "You're going somewhere for Christmas?"

"We're leaving for good, actually. Going back home."

He blinks in surprise. "Oh, I'm sorry to hear that. Have we done something wrong?"

"Oh, no, it's not you. We're going home for love."

A smile breaks Mark's normally stoic face. "Well, in that case, let me know how I can help."

"Can you drop this at the post office for us when I'm done and call us a cab for the airport?"

"Absolutely," Mark nods. "It would be my pleasure to."

I smile up at him as I finish packing the box. When it's done, he hands me a roll of a tape and a Sharpe marker. I don't know how he knew, but he came prepared. He's like a male Mary Poppins, only he's pulling things out of his jacket instead of a purse.

After the box is packed, I tuck it under my arm and check my watch. It's only two pm, but with traffic in New York, I'd rather be safe than sorry. "Ready, Joy?"

She slams her book shut and tucks it in her suitcase. "Ready."

Mark opens the door and leads the way to the elevator. As we wait for it to open, I hear Morgan's door open.

"What are you doing?" Her heels are clomping so hard as she stomps toward us that I can hear the sound even through the soft plush carpet.

"We're leaving, Morgan, and there's nothing you can do to stop us. You shouldn't have tried to control me." I place my hands on Joy's shoulder, pulling her closer to me.

Morgan sees the gesture and smiles. It's a vicious predatory smile that sends a chill down my spine. "I'll tell her who her mother is."

I'm about to respond when Joy pipes up. "I don't care who my birth mother is because she left me. Mothers don't do that. Presley is what a mother should be. She hugs me and reads me stories and plays with me."

Morgan's mouth drops open, but before she can reply, the elevator dings and we step inside, leaving Morgan standing in the hall catching flies.

"That was awesome, Miss Joy," Mark says softly, a smile tugging at his lips. "No one speaks to Miss Warner like that, but they should."

My own smile plays across my lips. I guess Joy got more than just my hair. In the lobby, Mark takes the package, gives Joy a high five, and wishes me luck. After thanking him, we step outside. A yellow cab waits at the curb.

I hold tight to Joy's hand as we march through the current of people to the edge of the sidewalk. Within minutes, a bright yellow cab is pulling over for us, and after placing our luggage in the trunk, we climb inside.

"Where to?" The man is foreign with a long scraggly beard, and his accent is hard to understand.

"The airport, please. American Airlines."

"You bet," he says, and the car pulls into traffic.

"Wait, can we make one stop first?" I give him the name of where I want to go, and the cabbie smiles in the mirror and nods.

Though my watch still shows plenty of time, the nerves have started taking root in my stomach, twisting and turning into a tightly coiled knot. My head is focused on Presley and what I'm going to say to her.

The car stops, and I glance around. We are stuck in the middle of traffic. I realize I hate traffic, yet another reason to get out of this city.

"Are we going to make it, Daddy?" Joy's face is pressed against the glass, and her voice is full of worry.

"We left early for a reason. We'll have plenty of time," I reassure her, but my own nerves are balling even tighter at the traffic.

Chapter Twenty-Six -
Presley

"Thanks for coming with us, Mom." I give my mother a hug before we throw on our coats to make the short trek to Brandon's parents' house.

"I'm just glad I could get the day off to spend with you guys," she says, returning the hug. There are tears in her tired eyes and more wrinkles than I remember on her face. Even her hair is grayer than it was six years ago. "I'm sorry I didn't get to spend more time with you children when you were younger."

"Don't be sorry, Mother. Yes, we would have loved to have you around more, but we understood the sacrifices that you made for us, and we love you even more because of it. I hope one day I'll get to be as great a mom as you were to us."

Ryan nods his agreement.

My mother smiles. "I have no doubt that you will my dear. If not Brandon, then some man will come along and make you a very happy woman."

I have my doubts in this small town, but I don't want to ruin the mood. Yesterday was lonely as Mother had to work. I kept the bakery open but only had two or three visitors all day. The evening had been spent watching sappy romantic Christmas movies on the screen with Ryan and wishing my life could be like theirs. I was looking forward to some festivities and people today.

We don't speak much on the short walk there, each lost in our own thoughts, but Anna makes up for it as we are ushered into the house.

"Here let me get your coats. Mom made gingerbread cookies, and they are delicious. Plus, she has a ham with all the fixings baking for lunch."

My smile is genuine as I hand over my coat. Part of it is based on Anna's verbal outpouring and part of it is based on the food. I remember missing that aspect in Paris. Though they had amazing food, it was often small portions and delicate dimensions, nothing like 'all the fixings' in Texas, which usually meant bread, potatoes, green bean casseroles, sweet potato pies, and more.

We follow her into the living room where Bruce is situated in the recliner in front of the television. The Cowboys are playing the Eagles today, and as he's a diehard fan, he'll be parked in front of the set until the game is over. For his sake, I hope the Cowboys win. I remember a few rough Christmases spent with Brandon when they lost, and everyone was in a sour mood for the rest of the night.

"Helena, Ryan, we're so glad you could join us," Beverly says, addressing my mother and brother as she enters the living room. The two women hug like long lost friends while Ryan waves and then plants himself on the couch to watch the game with Bruce.

"Thank you for inviting me. It seems I miss more of these gatherings every year, but now that Ryan has graduated, and I've started to pay down debts, I think I'll be taking more breaks."

"You'll have to promise to stop working so hard."

"You won't have to tell me twice. Is there anything I can do to help?"

The two women head into the kitchen leaving me staring at Bruce and Ryan and wondering what I should do.

"Presley, come help me finish wrapping some gifts," Anna calls from the family room.

Glad to have something to do, I join her. She is wrapping a large black box on the floor.

"Who is this for?"

"Dad," she answers, looking up just a second before returning her concentration to the paper that keeps falling off one side while she holds the other. Her sigh of exasperation sends her bangs flying into the hair before falling back to her forehead. "It's a tool box."

"Isn't it a little early for that?" I'm not trying to be rude, but Bruce is still using the walker to get around. I can't see him picking up this tool box anytime soon, but I drop to my knees and hold the side for her.

She shoots me a grateful look. "Yeah, that's what Mom said too, but I know Dad, and he's going to want to do something as soon as he feels normal again. This way it will be ready when he is."

"Sounds good." With my help, we finish the job quickly, though the wrapping job itself leaves a lot to be desired. Some of that is caused by the odd shape of the box though. It takes both of us to push it under the tree. As we do, my eyes land on a present addressed to Brandon.

"Is Brandon coming?" I ask Anna, hoping she'll say yes, even though I know the answer is probably no.

"No, that was just one we forgot to give him before they left."

"Oh."

"If it's any consolation," she says, seeing the emotion on my face, "Brandon can be pretty dumb sometimes, but he almost always comes around."

I flash her an appreciative smile, and then Beverly's voice carries down the hallway. "Girls, lunch is ready."

As we gather around the table, Beverly and my mother place the food on the table. Anna goes to the living room to help Bruce join us around the table, and I grab the cups and place them at the settings.

We have just sat down at the table when a knock sounds at the door.

"Who could that be?" Beverly asks, looking up.

"I'll go see." Anna bounds out of her chair to the front door.

Beverly starts the procession of food by scooping some potatoes onto her plate and then passing them to her right. She follows this with the ham and has just started the rolls when she gasps. I glance up to see her wide eyes staring at something behind me. I twist in my chair to see Brandon and Joy both smiling like loons. Anna stands beside them, as bewildered as her mother.

"Merry Christmas everyone. We're home." Brandon throws out his arms as if he's expecting us all to rush in for a hug.

"Well, I'll be," Beverly says. She drops the biscuit she had in her hand and rushes around the table to embrace them both. "What happened?"

"It's a long story," Brandon says, "but we have Presley to thank."

"Me?" What had I done?

"Yes, if you hadn't shown up and left those presents, we would never have known."

I stand up and cross to him. "I don't understand. If you saw them that day, why didn't you call me to come back?"

He shakes his head. "We didn't see them that day. Morgan hid them and didn't tell us you stopped by. Joy found them just yesterday, and I confronted Morgan. It seems she set the whole thing up – the promotion and everything."

"Oh, Brandon, I'm so sorry." As my words fade, I realize the rest of the family is watching in rapt silence. A blush spreads across my face.

"So, will you forgive us?" Joy asks.

"Of course I will. I should have known better. I never trusted Morgan."

Joy drops Brandon's hand and runs into my arms. Then the commotion commences. Beverly and Anna surround Brandon lavishing hugs and talking over each other. Even Bruce uses his walker to stand from the table and give Brandon a hug. Ryan stands, though he seems unsure what part to play — whether to be supportive or pull the brother card. I look up at Brandon over Joy's shoulder and smile.

After lunch, we gather around the tree. Brandon nods at the couch as he looks at me, the silent question evident in his raised eyebrow. Stifling a grin, I agree, and the two of us park on the couch, each taking one end. Joy climbs up between us, grabbing one of our hands with each of her own.

"Who's going to hand out?" Beverly asks. Anna finishes helping Bruce to the recliner and then sits in a chair beside him.

"I will."

Joy jumps up from the couch and pulls my hand so that I am forced to slide closer to Brandon. Laughing, he opens his arm, and I snuggle into it. His cologne wafts to my nose, woodsy and familiar. I have missed the smell of him and definitely the feeling of his arm around me. I catch my mother smiling at me from across the room where she is sitting and smile back.

Joy delivers the first present to Bruce, who opens it to reveal a new necktie. Beverly is next. She opens her gift to find a new pair of gloves. Joy delivers a gift to my mother next.

"Oh, you guys didn't have to do this," she says, but smiles as she opens the gift to find a beautiful scarf.

"Bug, get the one from my bag," Brandon says as Joy reaches under the tree. She pauses, then her eyes light up as she realizes what he means, and she hurries to the hallway where they must have left their suitcases. She returns bearing a small black box.

Brandon takes the box and slides from the couch to his knees in front of me. My eyes widen as I realize what he's about to do. "Presley Elizabeth Hays, I've loved you from almost the first moment we met, but I let my fear of losing you keep me from telling you. I didn't realize how much you meant to me until you came back into my life. I was a fool for not realizing the strength of what we have, and those few days apart from you in New York were the longest days of my life. The thought of losing you again ate me up inside, and I don't want to go through that again. I love you, and I'm asking if you will make Joy and I the happiest pair on Earth."

"Please Presley," Joy adds.

My eyes tear up, and my voice sticks in my throat, but I manage to nod. Brandon opens the box to showcase a beautiful diamond ring with a large carat in the middle and three smaller stones on either side. He slides it on my finger and then leans forward placing his lips on mine. The rest of the family erupts in clapping, and as Brandon pulls back, the pink I can feel on my face matches his own, at least what can be seen above his beard.

The rest of the present opening flies by, a blur to me as my mind is focused partly on the ring on my finger and partly on the man beside me. I'm still having trouble believing this is real as just yesterday I had resigned myself to possibly never seeing him again. When it's finished, Brandon grabs my hand pulling him up beside him.

"Take a walk with me?" His voice is low and throaty in my ear. The vibration of his whisper sends a shiver down my spine. I nod and follow him to the front door to grab our coats.

"I'm so glad you found it in your heart to forgive me," Brandon says as we step onto the porch.

"I wasn't mad, more confused. Seeing Morgan was a shock. I'm sorry I didn't call you back that night, but I couldn't figure out why you didn't say anything about her on the message. I guess I know now." Brandon's fingers intertwine with mine. It's a fit that feels like perfection.

He shakes his head. "That woman has some nerve. I can't believe she didn't think I'd find out or that I'd be okay with her trying to dictate my life."

"Is she gone out of your life for good?" I'm not afraid of Morgan anymore, but that doesn't mean I want to have to deal with custody battles or her coming into our life.

"Yeah, I think so. Joy kind of told her off. I don't think she was used to that."

My eyes widen. "She did what?"

He laughs and turns toward the park. "I'll tell you about it sometime. It was amazing."

"So, what are you going to do now? You're out of a job now, right?"

The large intake of his breath tells me he doesn't have it all figured out. "I don't know for sure, but I thought maybe I could use some of my promotion skills to put Sweet Treats on the map."

I stop in my tracks, pulling his arm so he is forced to stop as well. "Are you serious?"

His brows knit together in confusion over my actions. "Well, yeah. I think you could get online. Have orders to go, that sort of thing."

My eyes fill with water, and my lips purse together. "That would be amazing. I've been hanging on by a thread, and if I don't get some new customers soon, I'm not sure how much longer Sweet Treats will last."

"Why didn't you say anything?" He wraps his arms around me and pulls me closer. "I could have helped sooner."

I roll my eyes at him. He must have no idea how focused he was on his job. "You wouldn't have listened Brandon. You were too ready to get out of here."

His eyes cloud for a minute, and his teeth pull on his bottom lip. I didn't mean for the words to hurt him. "You're right. I was. I had tunnel vision and was only thinking about myself. Promise me that you'll help me keep from doing that in the future."

"I'll try, but you're a stubborn man, Brandon Scott." My hand brushes through his curly hair and trails down his beard.

"You're stubborn too, Presley Hays, but I'm glad of it."

As his hands tighten against my lower back and pull me forward, my arms slide behind his neck. His lips are soft and warm against mine. I had always thought people who said they saw fireworks when they kissed someone were full of it, but I can almost hear the explosions as his lips explore mine.

"Are you planning to stay here?" I ask when we pull back.

"Of course. In fact, I was hoping you'd go house hunting with me this week. I know you have your place until we get married, but I'd like to only buy one house and it makes more sense to have your input on it."

"I'd love that."

"Good, it's a date."

Chapter Twenty-Seven

- Presley

The parade of visitors begins promptly at seven the next morning as I open the shop. Paula, true to form, is the first one there.

"Is it true?" she squeals. "You must let me see it."

I hold out the ring as she oohs and aahs over it. "Paula, one day you will have to tell me how you always have the information before everyone else."

She smiles up at me. "I can't tell you that sweetie. It's a secret that will have to die with me, but I wonder if it will turn into a double wedding. I hear your brother and Anna are getting quite close as well."

I laugh and shake my head. "Whatever will you do when we all get married off?"

"Oh, there will be new people. Don't worry. If you succeed in getting this place noticed, I see many newcomers in our future. By the way, Shane at the realtor office asked me to drop these flyers off. He thinks some of these might be exactly what the two of you are looking for."

She places the papers on the counter and then heads for the exit, passing Brandon on his way in and issuing her congratulations to him as well.

"How does she know?" he asks as he sets his laptop bag on a table. He has offered to take pictures of the shop and begin working up a promotional website.

"I have no idea, but she even dropped these by." I hand him the flyers as we trade a quick kiss over the counter. I'd love for it to be longer, but I have a lot of baking to do today. Brandon wants pictures of all the pastries I make for the website and some of them are out of stock.

Shaking his head, he skims the papers, nodding at a few and frowning at others. I leave him to his work and begin grabbing the ingredients I will need from the back. The bell jingles as I return, arms laden with sacks and Tupperware containers.

"I'm so happy for you guys." Layla's voice carries in the small room.

"Thank you," Brandon says, and though he means it, I can hear the discomfort in his voice at being the center of everyone's attention.

"What's on your list today, Layla?" After freeing my arms from the load, I turn to the counter to get her list.

"Same as yesterday except for one thing. I want to see the ring."

I hold out my hand and enjoy the light that dances in her eyes.

"It's a good one," she says, winking at me.

"He's a good one," I say winking back. I fill up her order and wave goodbye as she exits.

"Is it like this every day?" Brandon asks from his chair.

"No, but it's not every day I get engaged either. You better get used to it. By my calculations, we have at least four more intrusions and that's not counting the regular patrons."

He sighs and rolls his eyes before turning back to his screen.

My estimations are nearly correct as by the end of the day Trudy, Max, Bert, Barnard, and Pastor Robert have all stopped in. I sink down in the chair next to Brandon, exhausted but happy.

"Let me show you what I've done." He pivots the screen, so I can see it better and shows me the webpage he has built. It is colorful and sweet and exactly what I would have wanted if I knew how to ask.

"It's amazing."

"Yeah, and here's the best part." He clicks off the webpage to some sheet filled with numbers. "If we can drive one hundred people to your site every month, and that's pretty small, you should see double the income you have coming in now."

The words and numbers on this page mean nothing to me, but I smile and nod as this obviously means something to him. His entire face lights up as he talks about the numbers, and I can see why he did so well in this job.

"So, shall we?"

"Shall we what?" My mind had zoned off as he was talking, and I had missed his last question.

"Shall we go and check out this house?" He places the page in front of me. The picture shows a quaint rambler with a wraparound porch. The siding is painted a pale blue and trimmed in white. A white rocker sits on the porch. I scan the details. 2200 square feet, four bedrooms, two and a half baths.

"It's amazing, but do we need something so large? There are only three of us."

His smile is mischievous as it stretches across his face. "For now, but you once asked me if I wanted more kids, and I can honestly say with you Presley that I hope we have a dozen."

I don't know whether to laugh or blush, so I do both. "Yes, let's go see it then."

We bundle up, and after locking the door, head home to grab Joy. After all, this house will be hers as well and we want her input. The house is a little further from the shop, but still a walkable distance.

The yard is large and fenced in with a white picket fence. "Daddy, look, there's a swing set in the back." Joy's voice rises in excitement as she drops our hands and runs to get a closer look.

Brandon's hand fills the void left from Joy's, and he smiles over at me.

The front door opens as we approach, and Shane, the local agent steps out on the porch. He is older than both of us with a Friar Tuck hairline but kind brown eyes. His long brown trench coat covers up whatever suit he is wearing underneath. Shane always dresses to impress. "Brandon, Presley, good to see you. Come on inside, and I'll show you around."

The front room is large and homey, painted a soft tan color that complements the brown in the hard wood flooring. A large cream-colored couch sits against one wall underneath a colorful painting. An overhead fan holds three light bulbs surrounded in frosted glass casings. Two ornate chairs sit on the other side of the room with a brown table between them. At the far end of the room is a large fireplace with a brick mantle.

"The furniture doesn't come with the place," Shane says, "but it helps you get the idea."

He leads the way out of the front room and into the kitchen. The colors are bright and airy, soft beige and cream. A travertine floor in a soft brown with silver specks runs throughout the room. The appliances are stainless steel, and a glass door opens to a large backyard. A slide and swing set stand in the yard.

"See, Daddy? See the swing set?"

"I see it, bug."

The dining room sits next to the kitchen and down the hall lies the bedroom and a hall bath as well as another living room. At the very back of the house is the master bedroom, painted a soft rose color with beige carpet. A queen four poster bed takes up a large part of the real estate in the room, but there is still room for a dresser and two nightstands. A large walk in closet and a master bathroom with a soaking tub complete the room.

"It's beautiful," I say, squeezing Brandon's hand.

"Yes, it is, but I'm afraid I need to get some money coming in first before going farther into debt. How long do you think it will stay on the market Shane?"

Shane purses his lips and scratches his balding head. "Don't rightly know. It's been up for a month, and I've only shown it twice. Best guess'd be another couple of months."

"Wonderful. I'll start crunching some numbers and looking for work, and we'll let you know."

The two men shake hands and we make our way back to the front door.

"Daddy, are we going to buy this house?" Joy asks, once again grabbing each of our hands.

"I hope to Joy, but we have to get some money coming in first. Now that I've quit my job, I'll have to find something here."

He is quiet as we walk back to his house to drop off Joy, and I know that not being able to provide for his family is weighing on him. I send a quick prayer heavenward for something to materialize for him soon.

Chapter Twenty-Eight
- Brandon

I close my eyes and then open them on the screen again. It can't be true. It's just not possible. "Presley, when you get a second, can you come here?" I lean back in my chair which sits just under the Eiffel Tower picture covering one wall in Presley's store.

"What is it?" she asks as she appears around the corner. Her hair is piled loosely on her head, and her purple streak — that adorable purple streak — has once again fallen out of place and hovers over her right eye. She blows it off her face and tucks it behind her ear as she approaches me.

"I want to show you something." I turn the computer to face her, and she sits down in the other chair. Her eyes scan back and forth across the page. She glances up at me, but I can tell she doesn't understand what she's seeing.

"Those are the orders that came in on your website this morning."

Her eyes return to the screen and widen as she takes in the page of emails. Her lips part, and her hand – nails painted a sparkly purple today – touches her mouth. "There's so many of them."

I laugh. "Yeah, thirty to be exact. You're only seeing the first twenty-five. There is another page."

"Thirty orders? How on earth am I going to bake that much?"

"Well, you have me, but I have the feeling you are going to need some help as well. If the orders keep coming in like this, and I have a good feeling they will, you are going to need a full-time helper."

"Brandon, this is incredible. I don't know what to say." The shock is evident in her voice as she struggles to find the words, a rare trait for Presley.

"For right now, I suggest we get started baking. I'll be your help today. Just tell me what we need to do."

A laugh escapes her lips. "Okay, let's get you an apron, and we'll start mixing."

While she heads to the back to grab an apron, I take the laptop and set it up on the table behind the counter, so we can see the orders while we're working. We spend the rest of the afternoon that way, mixing and baking and cooling and boxing up orders. Every once in a while, she leaves me to man the counter, but the customers are slow today, at least the in-store ones. The online orders continue to fly into the inbox faster than we can fill them.

"Do you think Anna would help? I know she's only home till school starts again, but we could sure use her help," Presley says, wiping her forehead with the back of her hand and leaving a white mark of flour in its wake.

I smile at her exhausted appearance and complete lack of knowledge of her smudge. She is so beautiful. "I'm sure she will as long as Mother can handle Joy alone."

Presley sighs. "Oh, that's right. I forgot she was helping your mom out during the day. I'd ask Ryan, but he burns toast. I suppose I better put out signs or take out an ad."

"I'm sure Bert could help you with that." It is meant as a joke, and Presley catches it, joining me in laughter as the image of Bert either baking with her or going door to door to find her a helper fills our heads.

"I'll talk to Rita at the Gazette tomorrow," Presley says when she manages to calm her laughter. The Star Lake Gazette is not a big newspaper, but Rita is a perfectionist and always puts out an amazing copy, and since it's the only newspaper in town, many of the residents still read it.

"That's a good idea. For now, I'm starving, so can we call it a night?" The clock on her wall reads six fifteen, past closing time, but I didn't have the heart to stop her in the middle of a batch of cookies. The over timer dings, signaling the last batch is ready.

"Let's box these up and get out of here," Presley says and while I take the cookies out of the oven, she locks the front door and turns the sign to closed. We finish packing up the cookies, perform a quick cleaning of the kitchen, and head over to my mother's house for a late dinner.

Ryan meets us at the corner of Cooper Street. He and Anna have begun hanging out together quite regularly and while they are not officially dating, I would give my blessing. I've always liked Ryan, not only because he was related to Presley, but because he always seemed genuine. It will be interesting to see how their story works out.

As we reach the porch, Joy comes out hollering. "Daddy, Presley, come see. Come see."

Unsure of what could have her so excited, we follow her into the living room to see my father slowly walking circles around the room, using only a cane. He looks up and smiles at us. "I've been practicing."

Presley and I both hurry to embrace him, and I hear Presley whisper, "Praise Jesus" as her arms encircle my father. I've never been as big of a believer as she has, but I'm starting to wonder if there is something to all of this. The bakery, my father, even my coming back all seem precipitated by prayers.

I ask Presley about her faith on the walk back to her apartment after dinner that night. She smiles and squeezes my hand as she tells me the entire story I only knew bits and pieces of. "I don't think I was doing the best I could," she says, "I wasn't practicing faith, but when you left, I knew I had to give it to God. Then I prayed for your father and for your job. I know you like to see things in person, but for me just seeing the things I prayed for come true is enough to make me a believer. I think if you would truly give your life to God, you would see amazing things happen as well."

Her words continue to rattle around in my head that night as I lay in bed staring at the white ceiling. I have nothing to lose and everything to gain, and I find myself whispering my own prayer before my eyes close for the night.

Anna accompanies me to the bakery the next morning. With my father able to walk more using his cane, my mother is freed up to watch Joy and insisted that Anna help. As it's New Year's Eve, I know Presley will want to close early and will probably stay closed tomorrow, so today is our shot to get as many of these orders taken care of as we can.

Presley is just opening the door as we arrive. "Oh, Anna, I'm so happy to see you. Not that Brandon wasn't a big help yesterday, but I kept having to differentiate between the flour, sugar, and salt for him." She smiles and winks at me.

"It's not my fault," I say, "I never claimed to be a chef."

"Baker," Presley says laughing. "Now, come on, we have work to do."

After a quick stealthy kiss, I release her and flip the sign on the window to open. The girls get the ingredients ready, and I set up the computer. I click on the website, and my jaw falls open. There are another fifty orders waiting for us.

"Presley, did you talk to Rita yet?" My voice is shaking with enthusiasm as I scan the page.

"Briefly, she said she'd come by this morning. Why?" Her voice carries down the hall from the back pantry.

"Because we're going to need that help soon."

The girls return, arms laden with ingredients.

"Holy cow, what is that?" Anna says as she sets down her Tupperware containers. Her eyes have found the computer screen.

"That is why you're here. We have another fifty orders."

Presley drops the bag she is holding, which thankfully was sealed though it lands with a thud on the table. "Fifty? We didn't even finish the orders from yesterday."

"Don't worry. I'll send emails to everyone letting them know there will be a slight delay due to New Years. You two just get to baking."

The girls begin mixing ingredients as I begin responding to each email. When that task is finished, I don my apron and help with the baking. With each jingle of the bell, Presley stops to help the customer, and I worry that we won't finish.

"Stop worrying," Anna says, poking my arm.

"I'm not," I say as I lay out some dough and begin running the rolling pin over it.

"You are too. Your forehead gets these frowny lines whenever you worry." She points at my forehead with her brown mixing spoon. The metal mixing bowl in which she is stirring cookie dough is cradled in her left arm.

I've always wondered how she knows. Anna, like Presley, has always been able to read my moods. Perhaps it is because of this tell I didn't even know I had. My hand reaches up to feel my forehead, but it feels the same way it always has. "Okay, so I am, a little. I just want this to go well for Presley." I want it to go well for another reason as well. If this takes off, we could afford this house and start putting money away for a nice wedding.

"It will. We're doing really well, and I have a few more days until I have to go back, so I can help out." She sets the bowl on the counter and cracks two eggs into it before stirring again.

"You're a good sister." I smile at her and reach for the raisins to sprinkle them into the cinnamon roll batter I have just rolled out.

Presley returns a moment later, a smile on her face. "Well, Rita has agreed to run an ad for us, but until it gets filled, her niece has just graduated and is looking for a job. I told her we'd try her out for a week, and if it works then we'll talk a full-time job."

"That's wonderful." I cross to Presley, gather her in my arms, and spin her around. She laughs as her loose hair flies about her head. When we stop, my hands slide down to sit on her hips. Her eyes stare into mine, and her breath catches. Every fiber in my body wants to kiss her, but we're in her shop and Anna is only a few feet away.

"Ahem," she says, clearing her throat, "I hate to interrupt you two lovebirds, but we still need to do some baking over here."

A soft pink blush, the color of carnations, spreads across Presley's nose and cheeks. With great reluctance, I remove my hands and return to my cinnamon rolls. Presley begins boxing up orders we have completed. By four in the afternoon, we have finished all but ten orders.

"Come on, Presley. We can always come back tomorrow to finish. Let's get ready for the dance," Anna says as she removes her apron.

Presley stares a moment longer at the order screen, sighs, and removes her apron as well. "Okay, I guess one more day won't hurt."

After she locks up, we walk her to her apartment before continuing back to my parent's house to change and get Joy. I feel like I haven't seen her the last few days, but she isn't angry about it as we enter the house. It must be this town and having family close.

"Daddy, is the dance tonight?" Joy asks as we enter the house.

"Sure is, bug. In a few hours. How was your day?"

"It was great. Come see what I did." She grabs my hand and pulls me into the living room where her little card table is set up. Finished, and taking up a good part of the table is the puzzle Presley got her for Christmas.

"Wow, Joy, did you do this all yourself?" Anna asks as she reaches my side and spies the puzzle.

"Well, mostly. Nana helped a little." Joy's voice is full of pride as she beams in front of the table.

"I guess it's time to get you an even bigger puzzle," I say as I ruffle Joy's hair.

Her eyes widen. "They get bigger?"

A small chuckle escapes my lips. "Yeah, they can get a lot bigger. I've seen a five-thousand-piece puzzle before."

"Five thousand pieces?" Her voice is barely louder than a whisper and dripping with awe.

"Yeah, maybe one day when we move into our house, we'll get a big puzzle and put it together. We'll need lots of floor space."

I leave her beaming and dancing and check on my father, who looks even stronger today. He is still using his cane, but not as much. Then I head to the shower to get ready for the dance tonight.

Chapter Twenty-Nine
- Presley

As the warm water sprays on my back, I rehash the events of the day. It is amazing to be baking again, though a little daunting. I can't believe how much business has picked up just from Brandon's webpage and whatever advertising he did.

I lather the strawberry scented shampoo into my hair and smile. I would never have imagined a year ago when I moved back here that Brandon would re-enter my life or that he'd propose, but I couldn't be happier. He is so much more relaxed working here with me than he was working for the promotional company in Dallas, and Joy completes a part of my life I hadn't even known was missing. Though the non-stop orders coming in are tough to complete now, my hope is they will allow us to purchase the house we toured and maybe put away a little for the wedding.

I haven't even begun planning it, but I hope that Brandon will be okay with it being a simple affair. I'd like to get a dress and a cake from out of town, and my hope is that Trudy will help decorate and Max will cater, but other than that, I have no grand plans. Just marrying him will be enough for me.

After washing the shampoo out, I turn the water off and step out amid a cloud of steam. I've always liked my showers short but hot. The steamy air always seems to clear my head, and I'd like to think it helps my skin, though that might just be wishful thinking.

I grab the purple terry cloth towel off the rack and dry off, wrapping it around my head when I'm done to soak up some of the water in my hair. The dance tonight is going to be more lowkey, so I pick a long-flowered skirt and matching shirt to wear.

With the clothing on, I dry my hair and apply just a dab of makeup. Eye liner to brighten my eyes, a tiny stroke of eye shadow across the lids, and a shimmery pink gloss. The image looking back at me from the mirror meets my approval, and I click off the light and head to the other part of the house for Ryan. We have agreed to walk together to meet up with Brandon, Joy, and Anna.

He is sitting at my mother's small kitchen table finishing a sandwich when I enter.

"You know, they're going to have food there," I say as I pull up a chair beside him and snag a chip off his plate.

"I know, but I'm starving, and this way I can focus more on Anna than filling my bottomless pit."

It's true. He has eaten several large meals a day since the time he was thirteen. I'd always thought it would taper off when he stopped growing, but evidently it hasn't. "Well, that was thoughtful of you. How are things with you and Anna anyway?"

His forehead wrinkles as his eyes cloud over. "They're good, I think, but I have to head back to Houston tomorrow. I don't know what the future holds for us."

"My suggestion is just enjoy tonight and don't worry too much about the next few months. If it's meant to be, it will work out."

"Yeah, though as you know," he says, pointing a finger at me, "that is easier said than done." He finishes the last bite of burger, and rinses his plate in the sink. "Shall we?" He holds out his arm and, with a smile, I place my arm in his.

We stop just long enough to grab our coats, and then we make our way toward Brandon's. He, Anna, and Joy meet us halfway, and we turn toward the barn. Along the way, we are joined by Max, who seems less grumpy today, and Layla, who is smiling in her naturally happy way.

The stars are out, and since the air is crisp and cold, the sky is clear, giving us a clear view of their brilliance. I squeeze Brandon's hand as we approach the barn. Music spills out of the open door, some country tune I don't recognize, but as this dance is for the whole family, I know there will be other songs coming soon.

As we step inside, I'm surprised to see the barn divided. To the right is Justin doing his DJ routine and blasting out the country music. A few couples, including Bert and Amelia are dancing. Bert's lime green suit elicits a small giggle, and I shake my head at his eccentricity. To the left, a pull down white screen is set up and an animated movie is playing for the younger kids. They are spread out on bean bag chairs and munching handfuls of popcorn. Across the back is a buffet table with hot dogs, hamburgers, chips, salads, and desserts. Just inside the door is a movable metal rack filled with coats and hangers. We shrug off our coats and add them to the group.

"I'll be by the food if you need me," Max says from behind me, but before he can make it to the table, Layla has snagged his arm, turning him back.

"No, you won't. You're going to dance with me." She winds her arms around his neck, and I watch as a slow crosses Max's lips. His arms encircle her waist, and he allows himself to be pulled to the dance floor.

"That looks like fun. Ryan, will you join me?" Anna holds out her hand, and Ryan, looking like he just won the lottery, puts his hand in hers and follows her to the dance floor. Anna's dark blue dress flares out as he spins her around before pulling her close.

"What about you Joy?" Brandon asks, bending down to Joy's level. "You want to dance with us or go watch the movie?"

Joy's lips purse, and she looks from right to left and back again. "I guess one dance with you, and then I'll watch the movie."

"Sounds like a plan," Brandon says, and with a wink to me, he leads her onto the dance floor. I step further into the barn to get out of the cold doorway.

"I hope he plans on saving you one."

I turn to see Trudy behind me, though I have to blink a few times to make sure it's her. Her dark hair is down and falling in soft curls at her shoulders. Her denim overalls have been exchanged for a denim skirt and bright red shirt that falls off one shoulder, revealing smooth brown skin underneath.

"Who are you? And what have you done with my friend Trudy?" I have never seen her in a dress, and the teasing jab escapes my mouth before I can stop it.

"Shut up. I just thought I'd see what all the fuss is about." She punches my arm lightly before folding her arms across her chest.

"Well, you look wonderful. You should do it more often. You could have the kind of love your grandmother had too, you know." I wiggle my eyebrow at her to emphasize my point.

She shrugs and together we turn back to watching the dancers. Brandon's face radiates pure happiness as he spins Joy around the floor. Anna's and Ryan's faces are nearly identical – the dopey starry-eyed faces of young love. Even Max's face, though serious, is focused on Layla, and the love between them is evident in his stare. I smile as I take them all in. This is the reason I love this town. These crazy characters who somehow still manage to find love and happiness in this small town.

"Would you look at that." Trudy's voice is quiet beside me, but I turn to see what she is looking at. Paula is entering the barn on the arm of Barnard. She is wearing a tight black dress and he is in a white suit with a black tie. They look more like they belong at a formal dance than our small town, but it is more surprising to see them together. I wonder if it is a new romance, just a friendly date, or a romance that has been going on in secret for some time.

"I guess there's someone out there for everyone. See, that means there's hope for you too." Trudy rolls her eyes at me, but there's a smirk on her face that leads me to believe that maybe, just maybe, she is rethinking her self-imposed ban on love.

"Sorry to interrupt," Brandon says, returning, "but may I have this dance?"

I look to Trudy to make sure it's okay. I feel bad leaving her alone when she's all dressed up and feeling vulnerable.

"Go, go," she says, waving her hand at me. "I'll go watch whatever is playing with Miss Joy for a bit."

As she takes Joy's hand and leads her to the left, Brandon grabs my hand and leads me to the dance floor. The music switches from an upbeat song to a slow ballad, and Brandon presses his right arm against my lower back, pulling me closer to him. With his left hand, he grabs my right, holding it against his chest. I can feel the beat of his heart through his shirt. My left arm glides up his shoulder, stopping just behind his neck.

"Did you ever think we would end up here?" His brown eyes are staring into my soul, and I find the words swimming in my head again.

"Not really, though I often dreamed about it."

"Me too." He spins us slowly around. "I'm so glad you didn't give up on me."

"I'm glad you gave me a reason not to."

As the music slows, he leans down just brushing his lips against mine. "More later," he whispers in my ear, and though I nod, it takes every bit of effort not to return the kiss now. My lips are tingling and craving another taste. "Let's get some food."

He steers us to the buffet table, and we pile our plates and then a plate for Joy. Walking carefully, to avoid spilling food, we make our way to the kids' side and find her snuggled in a blue bean bag chair. We deliver her plate, which she barely acknowledges as she is engrossed in the movie, and then return to the other side where a few tables are set up around the dance floor.

Anna and Ryan join us, their own plate brimming as well. I shake my head at Ryan's plate, which is filled from one end to the other as if he hadn't just eaten a few hours ago.

"Did Max do the food?" Anna asks, glancing around to see if he is close by.

Brandon takes a bite of his burger and shakes his head. "No, these aren't his burgers. Too dry. They must have had someone else bring the food in."

"Huh, wonder why?"

"Maybe Max didn't want to cook for all these people. It is a pretty big crowd." As I look around, it appears most of the town is here. Even Pastor Robert has shown up, though he is already dozing in the corner. Trudy is talking to a handsome man I don't remember ever seeing before. His black leather jacket gives him the air of a visitor. I'll have to ask her about him later.

"Maybe Bert brought the food over in his Lift service," Brandon says, chuckling at the thought.

"His what?" Ryan asks.

Shaking my head, I pull my gaze from Trudy and the unknown man. "You would have had to been here, but at the winter festival dance, Bert said he wanted to start a Lift service and taxi dogs around in his sister's car."

Anna's fingertips touch her forehead as she shakes it back and forth. "Ah, Bert, I'm gonna miss him when I go back to school."

"I'm going to miss a lot of things." Ryan's words are said solely in the direction of Anna, and as their gazes lock, I feel conspicuously like a third wheel, even though Brandon is sitting right next to me.

"Are we that bad?" I whisper in his ear.

"Worse," Anna says, and the four of us enjoy a chuckle.

After dinner, we check again on Joy, who has passed out in her bean bag chair. Trudy has wandered over to the adult side, and I wave as I see her chatting with Mr. Baker, the school principal. He's too old for her, but the fact that she is chatting with a man at all gives me hope that one day maybe she will take a chance on love.

Feeling the need to take a break from dancing until our food settles, Brandon and I find a deserted bean bag chair and plop down in it. It isn't exactly made for two, and neither of us get a very comfortable piece on our first try. After a little bit of shifting and a few different positions, we find one that works, and I curl into his arm.

As my head leans against his chest and his arm circles my shoulder, I find my eye lids slowly falling. It has been a long and busy day, and before I know it, I can barely lift them anymore. Hoping that Brandon won't be offended, I allow them to close and the world to go dark.

"Presley, wake up." Brandon's voice is reaching into my dream, and a hand is shaking my shoulder. Still heavy with sleep, I force my eyes open and look up at him.

"What is it?" My voice is slurry, and my throat feels fuzzy.

"It's nearly midnight," he says, stroking my cheek, "and there's no way I'm not kissing you on midnight."

His words push the invading sleep from my eyes, and I sit up. There's no way I want to miss midnight either. "How much time do we have?"

"Five minutes. Everyone is gathering to get some champagne."

"Then what are we waiting for?" I push myself up and hold out my hand to help him. Hand in hand, we stroll back to the adult side where Paula is ushering everyone to a table filled with fluted glasses. We join the crowd and snag a glass as soon as we are close enough to the table. Then we make our way to a more deserted part of the room and wait for the count to begin.

"Okay, everyone," Justin says into the microphone, "Happy New Year in ten, nine, eight...."

"Seven, six, five," we join in the count, "four, three, two, one. Happy New Year." Auld Lang Syne begins playing through the speakers, and after a quick sip of our champagne, Brandon takes my glass and sets it beside his on a nearby table.

"Presley Hays, I just know this is going to be the happiest year of my life. I love you," he says as his arms fold around me.

I smile, wrapping mine around his neck. "Brandon Scott, I have waited for this moment for seven years, and I can't wait to spend the next year with you. I love you more."

His lips form a smile before they part and press against mine. Heat flares through me as the passion between us ignites. This moment, this feeling is better than I ever could have imagined, and as the kiss continues, my heart warms at the knowledge that I will get to do this every day with the man I love for the rest of my life.

One month later

"Julie, I'll be back in a few hours," I say to Rita's niece, who I hired the day after New Year's. Her trial week had been more of a trial day, as she is a natural. Not only is she a great baker, but she is amazing with numbers and has helped me save money on my orders. I'd also had to hire Renee, a local high school student to help with the orders in the afternoon.

"No worries, boss. I have your cell if I need to reach you." Julie flicks a mock salute before turning back to her batch of cinnamon rolls. It's strange being called boss, but the perks are worth the oddity. With the money coming in, Brandon and I have been able to afford the house we looked at, and we signed the lease just yesterday. He and Joy will be moving in this weekend, which is good because Brandon has been having to rent a storage unit for his and Joy's things.

Joy started Kindergarten at the local school and Brandon uses that time to work on his business. Then he picks her up in the afternoon and they work puzzles together. So far, he has been great about keeping his work out of their time together, and they have grown closer than ever. With the success of Sweet Treats, he has reached out to other business owners and set many of them up online as well.

Even for those who didn't want an online presence, like Max, we have seen an increase in traffic to the town and all of us have seen business pick up.

The only thing still undone is planning for the wedding, but I've been so busy that I've let Trudy take over most of that. She has booked the venue, convinced Max to cater, and even taken care of the cake. The invitations Brandon and I took care of last weekend, so the last piece is the dress. I've agreed to take the afternoon off to go dress shopping with Trudy.

"You ready?" she asks as I open the passenger door of her blue mini cooper.

"Absolutely, let's get me a dress, so I can get married." I buckle the seatbelt and shift in the seat to face her. "You going to tell me about your mystery man yet?"

A smile pulls at Trudy's lips, but she shakes her head. "Not yet, but soon. I promise soon."

I want to press for more details, but I know Trudy. She'll tell me in her sweet time. For now, I lean my head back and smile because life is good.

The End

About the Author

Lorana Hoopes is a full-time teacher originally from Texas who now lives in the Pacific Northwest with her husband and three children. When not working, she can be seen at the gym, singing at her church, or acting on stage. She has five Christian romances out and a Children's series The Wishing Stone with more planned. She also hosts an internet TV show on TLBTV where she interviews authors to help them promote her books.

Be sure to check out her other books – The Power of Prayer, Where It All Began, When Hearts Collide, A Father's Love, Under the Mistletoe, Love Breaks Through, and The Wishing Stone books!

Made in the USA
Monee, IL
19 December 2023

49877797R00118